CRUEL CROWN

Also by Victoria Aveyard

Novels
Red Queen
Glass Sword

Digital Novellas
Queen Song
Steel Scars

CRUEL CROWN

QUEEN SONG
STEEL SCARS

VICTORIA AVEYARD

HARPER TEEN
An Imprint of HarperCollinsPublishers

HarperTeen is an imprint of HarperCollins Publishers.

Cruel Crown
Queen Song copyright © 2015 by Victoria Aveyard
Steel Scars copyright © 2016 by Victoria Aveyard
All rights reserved. Printed in the United States of America.

ISBN 978-0-06-243534-7 — ISBN 978-0-06-245627-4 (special edition)

Typography by Torborg Davern
15 16 17 18 19 PC/RRDH 10 9 8 7 6 5 4 3 2 1
❖
First Edition

CONTENTS

QUEEN SONG

As usual, Julian gave her a book.

Just like the year before, and the year before, and every holiday or occasion he could find in between his sister's birthdays. She had shelves of his so-called gifts. Some given in truth, and some to simply clear space in the library he called a bedroom, where books were stacked so high and so precariously that even the cats had trouble navigating the labyrinthine piles. The subjects varied, from adventure tales of Prairie raiders to stuffy poetry collections about the insipid Royal Court they both strived to avoid. *Better for kindling,* Coriane would say every time he left her another dull volume. Once, for her twelfth birthday, Julian gave her an ancient text written in a language she could not read. And one she assumed he only pretended to understand.

Despite her dislike for the majority of his stories, she kept her own growing collection on neat shelves, strictly alphabetized, their spines facing forward to display titles on leather bindings. Most would go untouched, unopened, unread, a tragedy even Julian could not find the words to bemoan. There is nothing so terrible as a story untold.

But Coriane kept them all the same, well dusted, polished, their gold-stamped letters gleaming in the hazy light of summer or winter's gray castings. *From Julian* was scrawled in each one, and those words she treasured above almost all. Only his true gifts were loved more: the manuals and guides sheathed in plastic, tucked between the pages of a genealogy or encyclopedia. A few held court at her bedside, snug beneath her mattress, to be pulled out at night when she could devour technical schematics and machine studies. How to build, break down, and maintain transport engines, airjets, telegraphy equipment, even lightbulbs and kitchen stoves.

Her father did not approve, as was the usual way. A Silver daughter of a noble High House should not have fingers stained in motor oil, nails chipped by "borrowed" tools, or bloodshot eyes from too many nights spent straining over unsuitable literature. But Harrus Jacos forgot his misgivings every time the video screen in the estate parlor shorted out, hissing sparks and blurred transmissions. *Fix it, Cori, fix it.* She did as he commanded, hoping each time would be the one to convince him. Only to have her tinkerings sneered at a few days later, and all her good work forgotten.

She was glad he was gone, away in the capital aiding their uncle, the lord of House Jacos. This way she could spend her birthday with the people she loved. Namely, her brother, Julian, and Sara Skonos, who had come specifically for the occasion. *Growing prettier by the day,* Coriane thought, noting her dearest friend. It had been months since their last meeting, when Sara turned fifteen and moved permanently to the Royal Court. Not so long really, but already the girl seemed different, sharper. Her cheekbones cut cruelly beneath skin somehow paler than before, as if drained. And her gray eyes, once bright stars, seemed dark, full of shadows. But her smile came easily, as it always did around the Jacos children. *Around Julian, truly,* Coriane knew. And her brother was just the same, grinning broadly, keeping a distance no uninterested boy would think to keep. He was surgically aware of his movements, and Coriane was surgically aware of her brother. At seventeen, he was not too young for proposals, and she suspected there would be one in the coming months.

Julian had not bothered to wrap her gift. It was already beautiful on its own. Leatherbound, striped in the dusty yellow-golds of House Jacos, with the Burning Crown of Norta embossed into the cover. There was no title on the face or spine, and Coriane could tell there was no hidden guidebook in its pages. She scowled a little.

"Open it, Cori," Julian said, stopping her before she could toss the book onto the meager pile of other presents. All of them veiled insults: gloves to hide "common" hands, impractical dresses for a court she refused to visit, and an already opened box of sweets her father didn't want her to eat. They would be gone by dinnertime.

Coriane did as instructed and opened the book to find it empty. Its cream pages were blank. She wrinkled her nose, not bothering to put on the show of a grateful sister. Julian required no such lies, and would see through them anyway. What's more, there was no one here to scold her for such behavior. *Mother is dead, Father gone, and Cousin Jessamine is blessfully still asleep.* Only Julian, Coriane, and Sara sat alone in the garden parlor, three beads rattling around the dusty jar of the Jacos estate. It was a yawning room that matched the ever-present, hollow ache in Coriane's chest. Arched windows overlooked a tangled grove of once-orderly roses that had not seen the hands of a greenwarden in a decade. The floor needed a good sweeping and the gold draperies were gray with dust, and most likely spiderwebs as well. Even the painting over the soot-stained marble fireplace was missing its gilt frame, sold off long ago. The man who stared out from the naked canvas was Coriane and Julian's own grandfather, Janus Jacos, who would certainly despair of his family's state. Poor nobles, trading on an old name and traditions, making do with little and less every year.

Julian laughed, making the usual sound. *Fond exasperation,* Coriane knew. It was the best way to describe his attitude toward his younger sister. Two years his junior, and always quick to remind her of his superior age and intellect. Gently, of course. As if that made any difference.

"It's for you to write in," he pressed on, sliding long, thin fingers over the pages. "Your thoughts, what you do with your days."

"I know what a diary is," she replied, snapping the book shut. He didn't mind, not bothering to be offended. Julian knew her better than anyone. *Even when I get the words wrong.* "And my days don't warrant much of a record."

"Nonsense, you're quite interesting when you try."

Coriane grinned. "Julian, your jokes are improving. Have you finally found a book to teach you humor?" Her eyes flickered to Sara. "Or someone?"

While Julian flushed, his cheeks bluing with silverblood, Sara took it in stride. "I'm a healer, not a miracle worker," she said, her voice a melody.

Their joined laughter echoed, filling the emptiness of the estate house for one kind moment. In the corner, the old clock chimed, tolling the hour of Coriane's doom. Namely, Cousin Jessamine, who would arrive at any moment.

Julian was quick to stand, stretching a lanky form transitioning into manhood. He still had growing to do, both up and out. Coriane, on the other hand, had been the same height for years and showed no sign of changing. She was ordinary in everything, from almost colorless blue eyes to limp chestnut hair that stubbornly refused to grow much farther than her shoulders.

"You didn't want these, did you?" he said as he reached across his sister. He snatched a few sugar-glassed candies from the box, earning a swat in reply. *Etiquette be damned. Those are mine.* "Careful," he warned, "I'll tell Jessamine."

"No need," came their elderly cousin's reedy whistle of a voice, echoing from the columned entrance to the parlor. With a hiss of annoyance, Coriane shut her eyes, trying to will Jessamine Jacos out of existence. *No use in that, of course. I'm not a whisper. Just a singer.* And though she could have tried to use her meager abilities on Jessamine, it would only end poorly. Old as Jessamine was, her voice and ability were still whip-sharp, far quicker than her own. *I'll end up scrubbing floors with a smile if I try her.*

Coriane pasted on a polite expression and turned to find her cousin leaning upon a bejeweled cane, one of the last beautiful things in their house. Of course, it belonged to the foulest. Jessamine had long ago stopped frequenting Silver skin healers, to "age gracefully" as she put it. Though, in truth, the family could no longer afford such treatments from the most talented of House Skonos, or even the skin healer apprentices of common, lesser birth. Her skin sagged now, gray in pallor, with purple age spots across her wrinkled hands and neck. Today she wore a lemon silk wrap around her head, to hide thinning white hair that barely covered her scalp, and a flowing dress to match. The moth-eaten edges were well hidden, though. Jessamine excelled at illusion.

"Be a dear and take those to the kitchen, Julian, won't you?" she said, jabbing a long-nailed finger at the candies. "The staff will be so grateful."

It took all Coriane's strength not to scoff. "The staff" was little more than a Red butler more ancient than Jessamine, who didn't even have *teeth*, as well as the cook and two young maids, who were somehow expected to maintain the entire estate. They might enjoy the candies, but of course Jessamine had no true intention of letting them. *They'll end up at the bottom of the trash, or tucked away in her own room more like.*

Julian felt quite the same, judging by his twisted expression. But arguing with Jessamine was as fruitless as the trees in the corrupted old orchard.

"Of course, Cousin," he said with a voice better suited to a funeral. His eyes were apologetic, while Coriane's were resentful. She watched with a thinly veiled sneer as Julian offered one arm to Sara, the other scooping up her unsuitable gift. Both were eager to escape Jessamine's domain, but loath to leave Coriane behind. Still, they did it, sweeping away from the parlor.

That's right, leave me here. You always do. Abandoned to Jessamine, who had taken it upon herself to turn Coriane into a proper daughter of House Jacos. Put simply: *silent.*

And always left to their father, when he returned from court, from long days waiting for Uncle Jared to die. The head of House Jacos, governor of the Aderonack region, had no children of his own, and so his titles would pass to his brother, and then Julian after him. At least, he had no children anymore. The twins, Jenna and Caspian, were killed in the Lakelander War, leaving their father without an heir of his flesh, not to mention the will to live. It was only a matter of time before Coriane's father took up the ancestral seat, and he wanted to waste no time doing so. Coriane found the behavior perverse at best. She couldn't imagine doing such a thing to Julian, no matter how angry he made her. To stand by and watch him waste away with grief. It was an ugly, loveless act, and the thought of it turned her stomach. *But I have no desire to lead our family, and Father is a man of ambition, if not tact.*

What he planned to do with his eventual rise, she did not know. House Jacos was small, unimportant, governors of a backwater with little more than the blood of a High House to keep them warm at night. And of course, Jessamine, to make sure everyone pretended like they weren't drowning.

She took a seat with the grace of one half her age, knocking her cane against the dirty floor. "Preposterous," she muttered, striking at a haze of dust motes swirling in a beam of sunlight. "So hard to find good help these days."

Especially when you can't pay them, Coriane sneered in her head. "Indeed, Cousin. So difficult."

"Well, hand them over. Let's see what Jared sent along," she said. One clawed hand reached out, flapping open and closed in a gesture that made Coriane's skin crawl. She bit her lip between her teeth, chewing it to keep from saying the wrong thing. Instead, she lifted the two dresses that were her uncle's gifts and laid them upon the sofa where Jessamine perched.

Sniffing, Jessamine examined them as Julian did his ancient texts. She squinted at the stitching and lacework, rubbing the fabric, pulling at invisible stray threads in both golden dresses. "Suitable," she said after a long moment. "If not outdated. None of these are the latest fashions."

"What a surprise," Coriane could not help but drawl.

Thwack. The cane hit the floor. "No sarcasm, it's unbecoming of a lady."

Well, every lady I've met seems well versed in it, yourself included. If I can even call you a lady. In truth, Jessamine had not been to the Royal Court in at least a decade. She had no idea what the latest fashions were, and, when she was deep in the gin, could not even remember which king was on the throne. "Tiberias the Sixth? Fifth? No, it's the Fourth still, certainly, the old flame just won't *die*." And Coriane would gently remind her that they were ruled by Tiberias the *Fifth*.

His son, the crown prince, would be Tiberias the Sixth when his father died. Though with his reputed taste for warfare, Coriane wondered if the prince would live long enough to wear a crown. The history of Norta was fraught with Calore firebrands dying in battle, mostly second princes and cousins. She quietly wished the prince dead, if only to see what would happen. He had no siblings that she knew of, and the Calore cousins were few, not to mention weak, if Jessamine's lessons could be trusted. Norta had fought Lakelanders for a century, but another war within was certainly on the horizon. Between the High Houses, to put another family on the throne. Not that House Jacos would be involved at all. Their insignificance was a constant, just like Cousin Jessamine.

"Well, if your father's communications are to be believed, these dresses should be of use soon enough," Jessamine carried on as she set the presents down. Unconcerned with the hour or Coriane's presence, she drew a glass bottle of gin from her gown and took a hearty sip. The scent of juniper bit the air.

Frowning, Coriane looked up from her hands, now busy wringing the new gloves. "Is Uncle unwell?"

Thwack. "What a stupid question. He's been unwell for years, as you know."

Her face burned silver with a florid blush. "I mean, worse. Is he *worse*?"

"Harrus thinks so. Jared has taken to his chambers at court, and rarely attends social banquets, let alone his administrative meetings or the governors' council. Your father stands in for him more and more these days. Not to mention the fact that your uncle seems determined to drink away the coffers of House Jacos." Another swig of gin. Coriane almost laughed at the irony. "How selfish."

"Yes, selfish," the young girl muttered. *You haven't wished me a happy birthday, Cousin.* But she did not press on that subject. It hurts to be called ungrateful, even by a leech.

"Another book from Julian, I see, oh, and gloves. Wonderful, Harrus took my suggestion. And Skonos, what did she bring you?"

"Nothing." *Yet.* Sara had told her to wait, that her gift wasn't something to be piled with the others.

"No gift? Yet she sits here, eating our food, taking up space—"

Coriane did her best to let Jessamine's words float over her and away, like clouds in a windblown sky. Instead, she focused on the manual she read last night. *Batteries. Cathodes and anodes, primary use are discarded, secondary can be recharged—*

Thwack.

"Yes, Jessamine?"

A very bug-eyed old woman stared back at Coriane, her annoyance written in every wrinkle. "I don't do this for my benefit, Coriane."

"Well, it certainly isn't for mine," she couldn't help but hiss.

Jessamine crowed in response, her laugh so brittle she might spit dust. "You'd like that, wouldn't you? To think that I sit here with you, suffering your scowls and bitterness for fun? Think less of yourself, Coriane. I do this for no one but House Jacos, for all of us. I know what we are better than you do. And I remember what we were before, when we lived at court, negotiated treaties, were as indispensable to the Calore kings as their own flame. *I remember.* There is no greater pain or punishment than memory." She turned her cane over in her hand, one finger counting the jewels she polished every night. Sapphires, rubies, emeralds, and a single diamond. Given by suitors or friends or family, Coriane did not know. But they were Jessamine's treasure, and her eyes glittered like the gems. "Your father will be lord of House Jacos, and your brother after him. That leaves you in need of a lord of your own. Lest you wish to stay here forever?"

Like you. The implication was clear, and somehow Coriane found she could not speak around the sudden lump in her throat. She could only shake her head. *No, Jessamine, I do not want to stay here. I don't want to be you.*

"Very good," Jessamine said. Her cane thwacked once more. "Let's begin for the day."

Later that evening, Coriane sat down to write. Her pen flew across the pages of Julian's gift, spilling ink as a knife would blood. She wrote of everything. Jessamine, her father, Julian. The sinking feeling that her brother would abandon her to navigate the coming hurricane alone. He had Sara now. She'd caught them kissing before dinner, and while she smiled, pretending to laugh, pretending to be pleased by their flushes and stuttered explanations, Coriane quietly despaired. *Sara was my best friend. Sara was the only thing that belonged to me.* But no longer. Just like Julian, Sara would drift away, until Coriane was left with only the dust of a forgotten home and a forgotten life.

Because no matter what Jessamine said, how she preened and lied about Coriane's so-called prospects, there was nothing to be done. *No one will marry me, at least no one I want to marry.* She despaired of it and accepted it in the same turn. *I will never leave this place,* she wrote. *These golden walls will be my tomb.*

Jared Jacos received two funerals.

The first was at court in Archeon, on a spring day hazy with rain. The second would be a week after, at the estate in Aderonack. His body would join the family tomb and rest in a marble sepulcher paid for with one of the jewels from Jessamine's cane. The emerald had been sold off to a gem merchant in East Archeon while Coriane, Julian, and their aged cousin looked on. Jessamine seemed detached, not bothering to watch as the green stone passed from the new Lord Jacos's hand to the Silver jeweler. *A common man,* Coriane knew. He wore no house colors to speak of, but he was richer than they were, with fine clothes and a good amount of jewelry all over. *We might be noble, but this man could buy us all if he wanted.*

The family wore black, as was custom. Coriane had to borrow a gown for the occasion, one of Jessamine's many horrid mourning frocks, for Jessamine had attended and overseen more than a dozen funerals of House Jacos. The young girl itched in the getup but kept still as they left the merchant quarter, heading for the great bridge that spanned the Capital River, connecting both sides of the city. *Jessamine would scold or hit me if I started scratching.*

It was not Coriane's first visit to the capital, or even her tenth. She'd been there many times, usually at her uncle's bidding, to show the so-called strength of House Jacos. A foolish notion. Not only were they poor, but their family was small, wasting, especially with the twins gone. No match to the sprawling family trees of Houses Iral, Samos, Rhambos, and more. Rich bloodlines that could support the immense weight of their many relations. Their place as High Houses was firmly cemented in the hierarchy of both nobility and government. Not so with Jacos, if Coriane's father, Harrus, could not find a way to prove his worth to his peers and his king. For her part, Coriane saw no way through it. Aderonack was on the Lakelander border, a land of few people and deep forest no one needed to log. They could not claim mines or mills or even fertile farmland. There was nothing of use in their corner of the world.

She had tied a golden sash around her waist, cinching in the ill-fitting, high-collared dress in an attempt to look a bit more present-able, if not in fashion. Coriane told herself she didn't mind the whispers of court, the sneers from the other young ladies who watched her like she was a bug, or worse, a *Red*. They were all cruel girls, silly girls, waiting with bated breath for any news of Queenstrial. But of course that wasn't true. Sara was one of them, wasn't she? A daughter of Lord Skonos, training to be a healer, showing great promise in her abilities. Enough to service the royal family if she kept to the path.

I desire no such thing, Sara said once, confiding in Coriane months before, during a visit. *It will be a waste if I spend my life healing paper cuts and crow's-feet. My skills would be of better use in trenches of the Choke or the hospitals of Corvium. Soldiers die there every day, you know. Reds and Silvers both, killed by Lakelander bombs and bullets, bleeding to death because people like me stay here.*

She would never say so to anyone else, least of all her lord father. Such words were better suited to midnight, when two girls could whisper their dreams without fear of consequence.

"I want to build things," Coriane told her best friend on such an occasion.

"Build what, Coriane?"

"Airjets, airships, transports, video screens—ovens! I don't know, Sara, I don't know. I just want to—to make something."

Sara smiled then, her teeth glinting in a slim beam of moonlight. "Make something of yourself, you mean. Don't you, Cori?"

"I didn't say that."

"You didn't have to."

"I can see why Julian likes you so much."

That quieted Sara right away, and she was asleep soon after. But Coriane kept her eyes open, watching shadows on the walls, wondering.

Now, on the bridge, in the middle of brightly colored chaos, she did the same. Nobles, citizens, merchants seemed to float before her, their skin cold, pace slow, eyes hard and dark no matter their color. They drank in the morning with greed, a quenched man still gulping at water while others died of thirst. The others were the Reds, of course, wearing the bands that marked them. The servants among them wore uniforms, some striped with the colors of the High House they served. Their movements were determined, their eyes forward, hurrying along on their errands and orders. *They have purpose at least,* Coriane thought. *Not like me.*

She suddenly felt the urge to grab on to the nearby lamppost, to wrap her arms around it lest she be carried away like a leaf on the wind, or a stone dropping through water. Flying or drowning or both. Going where some other force willed. Beyond her own control.

Julian's hand closed around her wrist, forcing her to take his arm. *He'll do,* she thought, and a cord of tension relaxed in her. *Julian will keep me here.*

Later on, she recorded little of the official funeral in her diary, long spattered with ink splotches and cross outs. Her spelling was improving though, as was her penmanship. She wrote nothing of Uncle Jared's body, his skin whiter than the moon, drained of blood by the embalming process. She did not record how her father's lip quivered, betraying the pain he truly felt for his brother's death. Her writings were not of the way the rain stopped, just long enough for the ceremony, or the crowd of lords who came to pay their respects. She did not even bother to mention the king's presence, or that of his son, Tiberias, who brooded with dark brows and an even darker expression.

Uncle is gone, she wrote instead of all this. *And somehow, in some way, I envy him.*

As always, she tucked the diary away when she was finished, hiding it beneath the mattress of her bedchamber with the rest of her treasures. Namely, a little pallet of tools. Jealously guarded, taken from the abandoned gardener's shed back home. Two screwdrivers, a delicate hammer, one set of needle-nose pliers, and a wrench rusted almost beyond use. *Almost.* There was a coil of spindly wire as well, carefully drawn from an ancient lamp in the corner that no one would miss. Like the estate, the Jacos town house in West Archeon was a decaying place. And damp, too, in the middle of the rainstorm, giving the old walls the feel of a dripping cave.

She was still wearing her black dress and gold sash, with what she told herself were raindrops clinging to her lashes, when Jessamine burst through the door. To fuss, of course. There was no such thing as a banquet without a twittering Jessamine, let alone one at court. She did her best to make Coriane as presentable as possible with the meager time and means available, as if her life depended upon it. *Perhaps it does. Whatever life she holds dear. Perhaps the court is in need of another etiquette instructor for the noble children, and she thinks performing miracles with me will win her the position.*

Even Jessamine wants to leave.

"There now, none of this," Jessamine muttered, swiping at Coriane's tears with a tissue. Another swipe, this time with a chalky black pencil, to make her eyes stand out. Purple-blue rouge along her cheeks, giving her the illusion of bone structure. Nothing on the lips, for Coriane had never mastered the art of not getting lipstick on her teeth or water glass. "I suppose it will do."

"Yes, Jessamine."

As much as the old woman delighted in obedience, Coriane's manner gave her pause. The girl was sad, clearly, in the wake of the funeral. "What's the matter, child? Is it the dress?"

I don't care about faded black silks or banquets or this vile court. I don't care about any of it. "Nothing at all, Cousin. Just hungry, I suppose." Coriane reached for the easy escape, throwing one flaw to Jessamine to hide another.

"Mercy upon your appetite," she replied, rolling her eyes. "Remember, you must eat daintily, like a bird. There should always be food on your plate. Pick, pick, *pick*—"

Pick pick pick. The words felt like sharp nails drumming on Coriane's skull. But she forced a smile all the same. It bit at the corners of her mouth, hurting just as much as the words and the rain and the falling sensation that had followed her since the bridge.

Downstairs, Julian and their father were already waiting, huddled close to a smoky fire in the hearth. Their suits were identical, black with pale golden sashes across their chests from shoulder to hip. Lord Jacos tentatively touched the newly acquired pin stuck in his sash—a beaten gold square as old as his house. Nothing compared to the gems, medallions, and badges of the other governors, but enough for this moment.

Julian caught Coriane's eye, beginning to wink for her benefit, but her downcast air stopped him cold. He kept close to her all the way to the banquet, holding her hand in the rented transport, and then her arm as they crossed through the great gates of Caesar's Square. Whitefire Palace, their destination, sprawled to their left, dominating the south side of the tiled Square now busy with nobles.

Jessamine buzzed with excitement, despite her age, and made sure to smile and nod at everyone who passed. She even waved, letting the flowing sleeves of her black and gold gown glide through the air.

Communicating with clothes, Coriane knew. *How utterly stupid. Just like the rest of this dance that will end with the further disgrace and downfall of House Jacos. Why delay the inevitable? Why play at a game we can't hope to compete in?* She could not fathom it. Her brain knew circuitry better than high society, and despaired at ever understanding the latter. There was no reason to the court of Norta, or even her own family. Even Julian.

"I know what you asked of Father," she muttered, careful to keep her chin tucked against his shoulder. His jacket muffled her voice, but not enough for him to claim he couldn't hear her.

His muscles tightened beneath her. "Cori—"

"I must admit, I don't quite understand. I thought—" Her voice caught. "I thought you would want to be with Sara, now that we'll have to move to court."

You asked to go to Delphie, to work with the scholars and excavate ruins rather than learn lordship at Father's right hand. Why would you do that? Why, Julian? And the worst question of all, the one she didn't have the strength to ask—*how could you leave me too?*

Her brother heaved a long sigh and tightened his grip. "I did—I *do.* But—"

"But? Has something happened?"

"No, nothing at all. Good or bad," he added, and she could hear the hint of a smile in his voice. "I just know she won't leave court if I'm here with Father. I can't do that to her. This place—I won't trap her here in this pit of snakes."

Coriane felt a pang of sorrow for her brother and his noble, selfless, stupid heart. "You'd let her go to the front, then."

"There's no *let* where I'm concerned. She should be able to make her own decisions."

"And if her father, Lord Skonos, disagrees?" *As he surely will.*

"Then I'll marry her as planned and bring her to Delphie with me."

"Always a plan with you."

"I certainly try."

Despite the swell of happiness—her brother and best friend *married*—the familiar ache tugged at Coriane's insides. *They'll be together, and you left alone.*

Julian's fingers squeezed her own suddenly, warm despite the misting rain. "And of course, I'll send for you as well. You think I'd leave you to face the Royal Court with no one but Father and Jessamine?" Then he kissed her cheek and winked. "Think a bit better of me, Cori."

For his sake, she forced a wide, white grin that flashed in the lights of the palace. She felt none of its gleam. *How can Julian be so smart and so stupid at the same time?* It puzzled and saddened her in succession. Even if their father agreed to let Julian go to study in Delphie, Coriane would never be allowed to do the same. She was no great intellect, charmer, beauty, or warrior. Her usefulness lay in marriage, in alliance, and there were none to be found in her brother's books or protection.

Whitefire was done up in the colors of House Calore, black and red and royal silver from every alabaster column. The windows winked with inner light, and sounds of a roaring party filtered from the grand entrance, manned by the king's own Sentinel guards in their flaming robes and masks. As she passed them, still clutching Julian's hand, Coriane felt less like a lady, and more like a prisoner being led into her cell.

Coriane did her best to *pick pick pick* at her meal.

She also debated pocketing a few gold-inlaid forks. If only House Merandus did not face them across the table. They were whispers, all of them, mind readers who probably knew Coriane's intentions as well as she did. Sara told her she should be able to feel it, to notice if one of them poked into her head, and she kept rigid, on edge, trying to be mindful of her own brain. It made her silent and white-faced, staring intensely at her plate of pulled-apart and uneaten food.

Julian tried to distract, as did Jessamine, though she did so unintentionally. All but falling over herself to compliment Lord and Lady Merandus on everything from their matching outfits (a suit for the lord and gown for the lady, both shimmering like a blue-black sky of stars) to the profits of their ancestral lands (mostly in Haven, including the techie slum of Merry Town, a place Coriane knew was hardly merry). The Merandus brood seemed intent on ignoring House Jacos as best they could, keeping their attentions on themselves and the raised banquet table where the royals ate. Coriane could not help but steal a glance at them as well.

Tiberias the Fifth, King of Norta, was in the center naturally, sitting tall and lean in his ornate chair. His black dress uniform was slashed with crimson silk and silver braid, all meticulously perfect and in place. He was a beautiful man, more than handsome, with eyes of liquid gold and cheekbones to make poets weep. Even his beard, regally speckled with gray, was neatly razored to an edged perfection. According to Jessamine, his Queenstrial was a bloodbath of warring ladies vying to be his queen. None seemed to mind that the king would never love them. They only wanted to mother his children, keep his confidence, and earn a crown of their own. Queen Anabel, an oblivion of House Lerolan, did just that. She sat on the king's left, her smile curling, eyes on her only son. Her military uniform was open at the neck, revealing a firestorm of jewels at her throat, red and orange and yellow as the explosive ability she possessed. Her crown was small but difficult to ignore—black gems that winked every time she moved, set into a thick band of rose gold.

The king's paramour wore a similar band on his head, though the gemstones were absent from this crown. He didn't seem to mind, his smile fiercely bright while his fingers intertwined with the king's. Prince Robert of House Iral. He had not a drop of royal blood, but held the title for decades at the king's orders. Like the queen, he wore a riot of gems, blue and red in his house colors, made more striking by his black dress uniform, long ebony hair, and flawless bronze skin. His laugh was musical, and it carried over the many voices echoing through the banquet hall. Coriane thought he had a kind look—a strange thing for one so long at court. It comforted her a little, until she noticed his own house seated next to him, all of them sharp and stern, with darting eyes and feral smiles. She tried to remember their names, but knew only one—his sister, Lady Ara, the head of House Iral, seeming it in every inch. As if she sensed her gaze, Ara's dark eyes flashed to Coriane's, and she had to look elsewhere.

To the prince. Tiberias the Sixth one day, but only Tiberias now. A teenager, Julian's age, with the shadow of his father's beard splotched unevenly across his jaw. He favored wine, judging by the empty glass hastily being refilled and the silver blush blooming across his cheeks. She remembered him at her uncle's funeral, a dutiful son standing stoic by a grave. Now he grinned easily, trading jokes with his mother.

His eyes caught hers for a moment, glancing over Queen Anabel's shoulder to lock on to the Jacos girl in an old dress. He nodded quickly, acknowledging her stare, before returning to his antics and his wine.

"I can't believe she allows it," said a voice across the table.

Coriane turned to find Elara Merandus also staring at the royals, her keen and angled eyes narrowed in distaste. Like her parents', Elara's outfit sparkled, dark blue silk and studded white gems, though she wore a wrapped blouse with slashed, cape sleeves instead of a gown. Her hair was long, violently straight, falling in an ash curtain of blond over one shoulder, revealing an ear studded with crystal brilliance. The rest of her was just as meticulously perfect. Long dark lashes, skin more pale and flawless than porcelain, with the grace of something polished and pruned into court perfection. Already self-conscious, Coriane tugged at the golden sash around her waist. She wished nothing more than to walk out of the hall and all the way back to the town house.

"I'm speaking to you, Jacos."

"Forgive me if I'm surprised," Coriane replied, doing her best to keep her voice even. Elara was not known for her kindness, or much else for that matter. Despite being the daughter of a ruling lord, Coriane realized she knew little of the whisper girl. "What are you talking about?"

Elara rolled bright blue eyes with the grace of a swan. "The queen, of course. I don't know how she stands to share a table with her husband's whore, much less his family. It's an insult, plain as day."

Again, Coriane glanced at Prince Robert. His presence seemed to soothe the king, and if the queen truly minded, she didn't show it. As she watched, all three crowned royals were whispering together in gentle conversation. But the crown prince and his wineglass were gone.

"*I* wouldn't allow it," Elara continued, pushing her plate away. It was empty, eaten clean. *At least she has spine enough to eat her food.* "And it would be my house sitting up there, not his. It's the queen's right and no one else's."

So she'll be competing in Queenstrial, then.

"Of course I will."

Fear snapped through Coriane, chilling her. *Did she—?*

"Yes." A wicked smile spread across Elara's face.

It burned something in Coriane and she nearly fell back in shock. She felt nothing, not even a brush inside her head, no indication that Elara was listening to her thoughts. "I—" she sputtered. "Excuse me." Her legs felt foreign as she stood, wobbly from sitting through thirteen courses. But still under her own power, thankfully. *Blank blank blank blank,* she thought, picturing white walls and white paper and white nothing in her head. Elara only watched, giggling into her hand.

"Cori—?" she heard Julian say, but he didn't stop her. Neither did Jessamine, who would not want to cause a scene. And her father didn't notice at all, more engrossed in something Lord Provos was saying.

Blank blank blank blank.

Her footsteps were even, not too fast or too slow. *How far away must I be?*

Farther, said Elara's sneering purr in her head. She nearly tripped over at the sensation. The voice echoed in everything around and in her, windows to bone, from the chandeliers overhead to the blood pounding in her ears. *Farther, Jacos.*

Blank blank blank blank.

She did not realize she was whispering the words to herself, fervent as a prayer, until she was out of the banquet hall, down a passage, and through an etched glass door. A tiny courtyard rose around her, smelling of rain and sweet flowers.

"Blank blank blank blank," she mumbled once more, moving deeper into the garden. Magnolia trees twisted in an arch, forming a crown of white blossoms and rich green leaves. It was barely raining anymore, and she moved closer to the trees for shelter from the final drippings of the storm. It was chillier than she expected, but Coriane welcomed it. Elara echoed no longer.

Sighing, she sank down onto a stone bench beneath the grove. Its touch was colder still and she wrapped her arms around herself.

"I can help with that," said a deep voice, the words slow and plodding.

Coriane whirled, wide-eyed. She expected Elara haunting her, or Julian, or Jessamine to scold her abrupt exit. The figure standing a few feet away was clearly not any of them.

"Your Highness," Coriane said, jumping to her feet so she could bow properly.

The crown prince Tiberias stood over her, pleasant in the darkness, a glass in one hand and a half-empty bottle in the other. He let her go through the motions and kindly said nothing of her poor form.

"That'll do," he finally said, motioning for her to stand.

She did as commanded with all haste, straightening up to face him. "Yes, Your Highness."

"Would you care for a glass, my lady?" he said, though he was already filling the cup. No one was foolish enough to refuse an offer from a prince of Norta. "It's not a coat, but it will warm you well enough. Pity there's no whiskey at these functions."

Coriane forced a nod. "Pity, yes," she echoed, never having tasted the bite of brown liquor. With shaking hands, she took the full glass, her fingers brushing his for a moment. His skin was warm as a stone in the sun, and she was struck by the need to hold his hand. Instead, she drank deep of the red wine.

He matched her, albeit sipping straight from the bottle. *How crude,* she thought, watching his throat bob as he swallowed. *Jessamine would skin me if I did that.*

The prince did not sit next to her, but maintained his distance, so that she could only feel the ghost of his warmth. Enough to know his blood ran hot even in the damp. She wondered how he managed to wear a trim suit without sweating right through it. Part of her wished he would sit, only so she could enjoy the secondhand heat of his abilities. But that would be improper, on both their parts.

"You're the niece of Jarred Jacos, yes?" His tone was polite, well trained. An etiquette coach probably followed him since birth. Again, he did not wait for an answer to his question. "My condolences, of course."

"Thank you. My name is Coriane," she offered, realizing he would not ask. *He only asks what he already knows the answer to.*

He dipped his head in acknowledgment. "Yes. And I won't make fools of both of us by introducing myself."

In spite of propriety, Coriane felt herself smile. She sipped at the wine again, not knowing what else to do. Jessamine had not given her much instruction on conversing with royals of House Calore, let alone the future king. *Speak when spoken to* was all she could recall, so she kept her lips pressed together so tightly they formed a thin line.

Tiberias laughed openly at the sight. He was maybe a little drunk, and entirely amused. "Do you know how annoying it is to have to lead *every single conversation*?" He chuckled. "I talk to Robert and my parents more than anyone else, simply because it's easier than extracting words from other people."

How wretched for you, she snapped in her head. "That sounds awful," she said as demurely as she could. "Perhaps when you're king, you can make some changes to the etiquette of court?"

"Sounds exhausting," he muttered back around swigs of wine. "And unimportant, in the scheme of things. There's a war on, in case you haven't noticed."

He was right. The wine did warm her a bit. "A war?" she said. "Where? When? I've heard nothing of this."

The prince whipped to face her quickly, only to find Coriane smirking a little at his reaction. He laughed again, and tipped the bottle at her. "You had me for a second there, Lady Jacos."

Still grinning, he moved to the bench, sitting next to her. Not close enough to touch, but Coriane still went stock-still, her playful edge forgotten. He pretended not to notice. She tried her best to remain calm and poised.

"So I'm out here drinking in the rain because my parents frown upon being intoxicated in front of the court." The heat of him flared, pulsing with his inner annoyance. Coriane reveled in the sensation as the cold was chased from her bones. "What's your excuse? No, wait, let me guess—you were seated with House Merandus, yes?"

Gritting her teeth, she nodded. "Whoever arranged the tables must hate me."

"The party planners don't hate anyone but my mother. She's not one for decorations or flowers or seating charts, and they think she's neglecting her queenly duties. Of course, that's nonsense," he added quickly. Another drink. "She sits on more war councils than Father and trains enough for the both of them."

Coriane remembered the queen in her uniform, a splendor of medals on her chest. "She's an impressive woman," she said, not knowing what else to say. Her mind flitted back to Elara Merandus, glaring at the royals, disgusted by the queen's so-called surrender.

"Indeed." His eyes roved, landing on her now empty glass. "Care for the rest?" he asked, and this time he truly was waiting for an answer.

"I shouldn't," she said, putting the wineglass down on the bench. "In fact, I should go back inside. Jessamine—my cousin—will be furious with me as it is." *I hope she doesn't lecture me all night.*

Overhead, the sky had deepened to black, and the clouds were rolling away, clearing the rain to reveal bright stars. The prince's bodily warmth, fed by his burner ability, created a pleasant pocket around them, one Coriane was loath to leave. She heaved a steady breath, drawing in one last gasp of the magnolia trees, and forced herself to her feet.

Tiberias jumped up with her, still deliberate in his manners. "Shall I accompany you?" he asked as any gentleman would. But Coriane read the reluctance in his eyes and waved him off.

"No, I won't punish both of us."

His eyes flashed at that. "Speaking of punishment—if Elara

whispers to you ever again, you show her the same courtesy."

"How—how did you know it was her?"

A storm cloud of emotions crossed his face, most of them unknown to Coriane. But she certainly recognized anger.

"She knows, as everyone else knows, that my father will call for Queenstrial soon. I don't doubt she's wriggled into every maiden's head, to learn her enemies and her prey." With almost vicious speed, he drank the last of the wine, emptying the bottle. But it was not empty for long. Something on his wrist sparked, a starburst of yellow and white. It ignited into flame inside the glass, burning the last drops of alcohol in its green cage. "I'm told her technique is precise, almost perfect. You won't feel her if she doesn't want you to."

Coriane tasted bile at the back of her mouth. She focused on the flame in the bottle, if only to avoid Tiberias's gaze. As she watched, the heat cracked the glass, but it did not shatter. "Yes," she said hoarsely. "It feels like nothing."

"Well, you're a singer, aren't you?" His voice was suddenly harsh as his flame, a sharp, sickly yellow behind green glass. "Give her a taste of her own medicine."

"I couldn't possibly. I don't have the skill. And besides, there are laws. We don't use ability against our own, outside the proper channels—"

This time, his laugh was hollow. "And is Elara Merandus following that law? She hits you, you hit her back, Coriane. That's the way of my kingdom."

"It isn't your kingdom yet," she heard herself mutter.

But Tiberias didn't mind. In fact, he grinned darkly.

"I suspected you had a spine, Coriane Jacos. Somewhere in there."

No spine. Anger hissed inside her, but she could never give it voice. He was the prince, the future king. And she was no one at all, a limp excuse for a Silver daughter of a High House. Instead of standing up straight, as she wished to do, she bent into one more curtsy.

"Your Highness," she said, dropping her eyes to his booted feet.

He did not move, did not close the distance between them as a hero in her books would. Tiberias Calore stood back and let her go alone, returning to a den of wolves with no shield but her own heart.

After some distance, she heard the bottle shatter, spitting glass across the magnolia trees.

A strange prince, an even stranger night, she wrote later. *I don't know if I ever want to see him again. But he seemed lonely too. Should we not be lonely together?*

At least Jessamine was too drunk to scold me for running off.

Life at court was neither better nor worse than life on the estate.

The governorship came with greater incomes, but not nearly enough to elevate House Jacos beyond much more than the basic amenities. Coriane still did not have her own maid, nor did she want one, though Jessamine continued to crow about needing help of her own. At least the Archeon town house was easier to maintain, rather than the Aderonack estate now shuttered in the wake of the family's transplant to the capital.

I miss it, somehow, Coriane wrote. *The dust, the tangled gardens, the emptiness and the silence. So many corners that were my own, far from Father and Jessamine and even Julian.* Most of all she mourned the loss of the garage and outbuildings. The family had not owned a working transport in years, let alone employed a driver, but the remnants remained. There was the hulking skeleton of the private transport, a six-seater, its engine transplanted to the floor like an organ. Busted water heaters, old furnaces cannibalized for parts, not to mention odds and ends from their long-gone gardening staff, littered the various sheds and holdings. *I leave behind unfinished puzzles, pieces never put back together. It feels wasteful. Not of the objects, but myself. So much time spent stripping wire or counting screws. For what? For knowledge I will never use? Knowledge that is* cursed, inferior, stupid, *to everyone else? What have I done with myself for fifteen years? A great construct of nothing. I suppose I miss the old house because it was with me in my emptiness, in my silence. I thought I hated the estate, but I think I hate the capital more.*

Lord Jacos refused his son's request, of course. His heir would not go to Delphie to translate crumbling records and archive petty arti- facts. "No point in it," he said. Just as he saw no point in most of what Coriane did, and regularly voiced that opinion.

Both children were gutted, feeling their escape snatched away. Even Jessamine noticed their downturn in emotion, though she said nothing to either. But Coriane knew their old cousin went easy on her in their first months at court, or rather, she was hard on the drink. For as much as Jessamine talked of Archeon and Summerton, she didn't seem to like either very much, if her gin consumption was any indication.

More often than not, Coriane could slip away during Jessamine's daily "nap." She walked the city many times in hopes of finding a place she enjoyed, somewhere to anchor her in the newly tossing sea of her life.

She found no such place—instead she found a person.

He asked her to call him Tibe after a few weeks. A family nick- name, used among the royals and a precious few friends. "All right, then," Coriane said, agreeing to his request. "Saying 'Your Highness' was getting to be a bit of a pain."

They first met by chance, on the massive bridge that spanned the Capital River, connecting both sides of Archeon. A marvelous structure of twisted steel and trussed iron, supporting three levels of roadway, plazas, and commercial squares. Coriane was not so dazzled by silk shops or the stylish eateries jutting out over the water, but more interested in the bridge itself, its construction. She tried to fathom how many tons of metal were beneath her feet, her mind a flurry of equations. At first, she didn't notice the Sentinels walking toward her, nor the prince they followed. He was clearheaded this time, without a bottle in hand, and she thought he would pass her by.

Instead, he stopped at her side, his warmth a gentle ebb like the touch of a summer sun. "Lady Jacos," he said, following her gaze to the steel of the bridge. "Something interesting?"

She inclined her head in a bow, but didn't want to embarrass herself with another poor curtsy. "I think so," she replied. "I was just wondering how many tons of metal we're standing on, hoping it will keep us up."

The prince let out a puff of laughter tinged with nervous. He shifted his feet, as if suddenly realizing exactly how high above the water they were. "I'll do my best to keep that thought out of my head," he mumbled. "Any other frightening notions to share?"

"How much time do you have?" she said with half a grin. Half only, because something tugged at the rest, weighing it down. The cage of the capital was not a happy place for Coriane.

Nor Tiberias Calore. "Would you favor me with a walk?" he asked, extending an arm. This time, Coriane saw no hesitation in him, or even the pensive wonderings of a question. He knew her answer already.

"Of course." And she slipped her arm in his.

This will be the last time I hold the arm of a prince, she thought as they walked the bridge. She thought that every time, and she was always wrong.

In early June, a week before the court would flee Archeon for the smaller but just as grand summer palace, Tibe brought someone to meet her. They were to rendezvous in East Archeon, in the sculpture garden outside the Hexaprin Theater. Coriane was early, for Jessamine started drinking during breakfast, and she was eager to get away. For once, her relative poverty was an advantage. Her clothes were ordinary, clearly Silver, as they were striped in her house colors of gold and yellow, but nothing remarkable. No gems to denote her as a lady of a High House, as someone worth noticing. Not even a servant in uniform to stand a few paces behind. The other Silvers floating through the collection of carved marble barely saw her, and for once, she liked it that way.

The green dome of Hexaprin rose above, shading her from the still rising sun. A black swan of smooth, flawless granite perched at the top, its long neck arched and wings spread wide, every feather meticulously sculpted. A beautiful monument to Silver excess. *And probably Red made,* she knew, glancing around. There were no Reds nearby, but they bustled on the street. A few stopped to glance at the theater, their eyes raised to a place they could never inhabit. *Perhaps I'll bring Eliza and Melanie someday.* She wondered if the maids would like that, or be embarrassed by such charity.

She never found out. Tibe's arrival erased all thoughts of her Red servants, and most other things along with them.

He had none of his father's beauty, but was handsome in his own way. Tibe had a strong jaw, still stubbornly trying to grow a beard, with expressive golden eyes and a mischievous smile. His cheeks flushed when he drank and his laughter intensified, as did his rippling heat, but at the moment he was sober as a judge and twitchy. *Nervous,* Coriane realized as she moved to meet him and his entourage.

Today he was dressed plainly—*but not as poorly as me*. No uniform, medals, nothing official to denote this a royal event. He wore a simple coat, charcoal-gray, over a white shirt, dark red trousers, and black boots polished to a mirror shine. The Sentinels were not so informal. Their masks and flaming robes were mark enough of his birthright.

"Good morning," he said, and she noticed his fingers drumming rapidly at his side. "I thought we could see *Fall of Winter*. It's new, from Piedmont."

Her heart leapt at the prospect. The theater was an extravagance her family could hardly afford and, judging by the glint in Tibe's eye, he knew that. "Of course, that sounds wonderful."

"Good," he replied, hooking her arm in his own. It was second nature to both of them now, but still Coriane's arm buzzed with the feel of him. She had long decided theirs was only a friendship—*he's a prince, bound to Queenstrial*—though she could still enjoy his presence.

They left the garden, heading for the tiled steps of the theater and the fountained plaza before the entrance. Most stopped to give them room, watching as their prince and a noble lady crossed to the theater. A few snapped photographs, the bright lights blinding Coriane, but Tibe smiled through it. He was used to this sort of thing. She didn't mind it either, not truly. In fact, she wondered whether or not there was a way to dim the camera bulbs, and prevent them from stunning anyone who came near. The thought of bulbs and wire and shaded glass occupied her until Tibe spoke.

"Robert will be joining us, by the way," he blurted as they crossed the threshold, stepping over a mosaic of black swans taking flight. At first, Coriane barely heard him, stunned as she was by the beauty of Hexaprin, with its marbled walls, soaring staircases, explosions of flowers, and mirrored ceiling hung with a dozen gilded chandeliers.

But after a second, she clamped her jaw shut and turned back to Tibe to find him blushing furiously, worse than she had ever seen.

She blinked at him, concerned. In her mind's eye she saw the king's paramour, the prince who was not royal. "That's quite all right with me," she said, careful to keep her voice low. There was a crowd forming, eager to enter the matinee performance. "Unless it isn't all right with you?"

"No, no, I'm very happy he came. I—I asked him to come." Somehow, the prince was tripping over his words, and Coriane could not understand why. "I wanted him to meet you."

"Oh," she said, not knowing what else to say. Then she glanced down at her dress—ordinary, out of style—and frowned. "I wish I wore something else. It's not every day you meet a prince," she added with the shadow of a wink.

He barked a laugh of humor and relief. "Clever, Coriane, very clever."

They bypassed the ticket booths, as well as the public entrance to the theater. Tibe led her up one of the winding staircases, offering her a better view of the massive foyer. As on the bridge, she wondered who made this place, but deep down, she knew. Red labor, Red craftsmen, with perhaps a few magnetrons to aid the process. There was the usual twinge of disbelief. *How could servants create such beauty and still be considered inferior? They are capable of wonders different from our own.*

They gained skill through handiwork and practice, rather than birth. *Is that not equal to Silver strength, if not greater than it?* But she did not dwell on such thoughts long. She never did. *This is the way of the world.*

The royal box was at the end of a long, carpeted hall decorated by paintings. Many were of Prince Robert and Queen Anabel, both great patrons of the arts in the capital. Tibe pointed them out with pride, lingering by a portrait of Robert and his mother in full regalia.

"Anabel *hates* that painting," a voice said from the end of the hall. Like his laugh, Prince Robert's voice had a melody to it, and Coriane wondered if he had singer blood in his family.

The prince approached, gliding silently across the carpet with long, elegant strides. *A silk,* Coriane knew, remembering he was of House Iral. His ability was agility, balance, lending him swift movement and acrobat-like skill. His long hair fell over one shoulder, gleaming in dark waves of blue-black. As he closed the distance between them, Coriane noticed gray at his temples, as well as laugh lines around his mouth and eyes.

"She doesn't think it a true likeness of us—too pretty, you know your mother," Robert continued, coming to stop in front of the painting. He gestured to Anabel's face and then his own. Both seemed to glow with youth and vitality, their features beautiful and eyes bright. "But I think it's just fine. After all, who doesn't need a little help now and then?" he added with a kind wink. "You'll find that soon enough, Tibe."

"Not if I can help it," Tibe replied. "Sitting for paintings might be the most boring act in the kingdom."

Coriane angled a glance at him. "A small price to pay, though. For a crown."

"Well said, Lady Jacos, well said." Robert laughed, tossing back his hair. "Step lightly around this one, my boy. Though it seems you've already forgotten your manners?"

"Of course, of course," Tibe said, and waved his hand, gesturing for Coriane to come closer. "Uncle Robert, this is Coriane of House Jacos, daughter of Lord Harrus, Governor of Aderonack. And Coriane, this is Prince Robert of House Iral, Sworn Consort of His Royal Majesty, King Tiberias the Fifth."

Her curtsy had improved in the past months, but not by much. Still, she attempted, only to have Robert pull her into an embrace. He smelled of lavender and—*baked bread*? "A pleasure to finally meet you," he said, holding her at arm's length. For once, Coriane did not feel as if she was being examined. There didn't seem to be an unkind bone in Robert's body, and he smiled warmly at her. "Come now, they should be starting momentarily."

As Tibe did before, Robert took her arm, patting her hand like a doting grandfather.

"You must sit by me, of course."

Something tightened in Coriane's chest, an unfamiliar sensation. Was it . . . happiness? She thought so.

Grinning as widely as she could, she looked over her shoulder to see Tibe following, his eyes on hers, his smile both joyous and relieved.

The next day, Tibe left with his father to review troops at a fort in Delphie, leaving Coriane free to visit Sara. House Skonos had an opulent town house on the slopes of West Archeon, but they also enjoyed apartments in Whitefire Palace itself, should the royal family have need of a skilled skin healer at any moment. Sara met her at the gates unaccompanied, her smile perfect for the guards, but a warning to Coriane.

"What's wrong? What is it?" she whispered as soon as they reached the gardens outside the Skonos chambers.

Sara drew them farther into the trees, until they were inches from an ivy-draped garden wall, with immense rosebushes on either side, obstructing them both from view. A thrum of panic went through Coriane. *Has something happened? To Sara's parents? Was Julian wrong—would*

Sara leave them for the war? Coriane selfishly hoped that was not the case. She loved Sara as well as Julian did, but was not so willing to see her go, even for her own aspirations. Already the thought filled her with dread, and she felt tears prick her eyes.

"Sara, are you—are you going to—?" she began, stammering, but Sara waved her off.

"Oh, Cori, this has nothing to do with me. Don't you dare cry," she added, forcing a small laugh while she hugged Coriane. "Oh, I'm sorry, I didn't meant to upset you. I just didn't want to be overheard."

Relief flooded through Coriane. "Thank my colors," she mumbled. "So what requires such secrecy? Is your grandmother asking you to lift her eyebrows again?"

"I certainly hope not."

"Then what?"

"You met Prince Robert."

Coriane scoffed. "And? This is court, everyone's met Robert—"

"Everyone *knows* him, but they don't have private audiences with the king's paramour. In fact, he is not at all well liked."

"Can't imagine why. He's probably the kindest person here."

"Jealousy mostly, and a few of the more traditional houses think it's wrong to elevate him so high. 'Crowned prostitute' is the term most used, I think."

Coriane flushed, both with anger and embarrassment on Robert's behalf. "Well, if it's a scandal to meet him and like him, I don't mind in the least. Neither did Jessamine, actually, she was quite excited when I explained—"

"Because Robert isn't the scandal, Coriane." Sara took her hands, and Coriane felt a bit of her friend's ability seep into her skin. A cool touch that meant her paper cut from yesterday would be gone in a blink. "It's you and the crown prince, your closeness. Everyone knows how tightly knit the royal family is, particularly where Robert is concerned. They value him and protect him above everything. If Tiberias wanted you two to meet then—"

Despite the pleasant sensation, Coriane dropped Sara's hands. "We're friends. That's all this ever can be." She forced a giggle that was quite unlike herself. "You can't seriously think Tibe sees me as anything more, that he *wants* or even *can want* anything more from me?"

She expected her friend to laugh with her, to wave it all off as a joke. Instead, Sara had never looked so grave. "All signs point to yes, Coriane."

"Well, you're wrong. I'm not—he wouldn't—and besides, there's Queenstrial to think of. It must be soon, he's of age, and no one would ever choose me."

Again, Sara took Coriane's hands and gave them a gentle squeeze. "I think he would."

"Don't say that to me," Coriane whispered. She looked to the roses, but it was Tibe's face she saw. It was familiar now, after months of friendship. She knew his nose, his lips, his jaw, his eyes most of all. They stirred something in her, a connection she did not know she could make with another person. She saw herself in them, her own pain, her own joy. *We are the same,* she thought. *Searching for something to keep us anchored, both alone in a crowded room.* "It's impossible. And telling me this, giving me any kind of hope where he is concerned . . ." She sighed and bit her lip. "I don't need that heartache along with everything else. He's my friend, and I'm his. Nothing more."

Sara was not one for fancies or daydreaming. She cared more for mending broken bones than broken hearts. So Coriane could not help but believe her when she spoke, even against her own misgivings.

"Friend or not, Tibe favors you. And for that alone, you must be careful. He's just painted a target on your back, and every girl at court knows it."

"Every girl at court hardly knows who I am, Sara."

But still, she returned home vigilant.

And that night, she dreamed of knives in silk, cutting her apart.

There would be no Queenstrial.

Two months passed at the Hall of the Sun, and with every dawn the court waited for some announcement. Lords and ladies pestered the king, asking when his son would choose a bride from their daughters. He was not moved by anyone's petition, meeting all with his beautiful, stoic eyes. Queen Anabel was quite the same, giving no indication as to when her son would undertake his most important duty. Only Prince Robert had the boldness to smile, knowing precisely what storm gathered on the horizon. The whispers rose as days passed. They wondered if Tiberias was like his father, preferring men to women—but even then, he was bound to choose a queen to bear him sons of his own. Others were more astute, picking up the trail of carefully laid bread crumbs Robert had left for them. They were meant to be gentle, helpful signposts. *The prince has made his choice clear, and no arena will change his mind.*

Coriane Jacos dined with Robert regularly, as well as Queen Anabel. Both were quick to praise the young girl, so much so that the gossips wondered if House Jacos was as weak as they appeared. "A trick?" they said. "A poor mask to hide a powerful face?" The cynics among them found other explanations. "She's a singer, a manipulator. She looked into the prince's eyes and made him love her. It would not be the first time someone broke our laws for a crown."

Lord Harrus reveled in the newfound attention. He used it as leverage, to trade on his daughter's future for tetrarch coins and credit. But he was a poor player in a large, complicated game. He lost as much as he borrowed, betting on cards as well as Treasury stocks or undertaking ill-thought, costly ventures to "improve" his governed region. He founded two mines at the behest of Lord Samos, who assured him of rich iron veins in the Aderonack hills. Both failed within weeks, turning up nothing but dirt.

Only Julian was privy to such failures, and he was careful to keep them from his sister. Tibe, Robert, and Anabel did the same, shielding her from the worst gossip, working in conjunction with Julian and Sara to keep Coriane blissful in her ignorance. But of course, Coriane heard all things even through their protections. And to keep her family and friends from worry, to keep *them* happy, she pretended to be the same. Only her diary knew the cost of such lies.

Father will bury us with both hands. He boasts of me to his so-called friends, telling them I'm the next queen of this kingdom. I don't think he's ever paid so much attention to me before, and even now, it is minuscule, not for my own benefit. He pretends to love me now because of another, because of Tibe. Only when someone else sees worth in me does he condescend to do the same.

Because of her father, she dreamed of a Queenstrial she did not win, of being cast aside and returned to the old estate. Once there, she was made to sleep in the family tomb, beside the still, bare body of her uncle. When the corpse twitched, hands reaching for her throat, she would wake, drenched in sweat, unable to sleep for the rest of the night.

Julian and Sara think me weak, fragile, a porcelain doll who will shatter if touched, she wrote. *Worst of all, I'm beginning to believe them. Am I really so frail? So useless? Surely I can be of some help somehow, if Julian would only ask? Are Jessamine's lessons the best I can do? What am I becoming in this place? I doubt I even remember how to replace a lightbulb. I am not someone I recognize. Is this what growing up means?*

Because of Julian, she dreamed of being in a beautiful room. But every door was locked, every window shut, with nothing and no one to keep her company. Not even books. Nothing to upset her. And always, the room would become a birdcage with gilded bars. It would shrink and shrink until it cut her skin, waking her up.

I am not the monster the gossips think me to be. I've done nothing, manipulated no one. I haven't even attempted to use my ability in months, since Julian has no more time to teach me. But they don't believe that. I see how they look at me, even the whispers of House Merandus. Even Elara. I have not heard her in my head since the banquet, when her sneers drove me to Tibe. Perhaps that taught her better than to meddle. Or maybe she is afraid of looking into my eyes and hearing my voice, as if I'm some kind of match for her razored whispers. I am not, of course. I am hopelessly undefended against people like her. Perhaps I should thank whoever started the rumor. It keeps predators like her from making me prey.

Because of Elara, she dreamed of ice-blue eyes following her every move, watching as she donned a crown. People bowed under her gaze and sneered when she turned away, plotting against their newly made queen. They feared her and hated her in equal measure, each one a wolf waiting for her to be revealed as a lamb. She sang in the dream, a wordless song that did nothing but double their bloodlust. Sometimes they killed her, sometimes they ignored her, sometimes they put her in a cell. All three wrenched her from sleep.

Today Tibe said he loves me, that he wants to marry me. I do not believe him. Why would he want such a thing? I am no one of consequence. No great beauty or intellect, no strength or power to aid his reign. I bring nothing to him but worry and weight. He needs someone strong at his side, a person who laughs at the gossips and overcomes her own doubts. Tibe is as weak as I am, a lonely boy without a path of his own. I will only make things worse. I will only bring him pain. How can I do that?

Because of Tibe, she dreamed of leaving court for good. Like Julian wanted to do, to keep Sara from staying behind. The locations varied with the changing nights. She ran to Delphie or Harbor Bay or Piedmont or even the Lakelands, each one painted in shades of black and gray. Shadow cities to swallow her up and hide her from the prince and the crown he offered. But they frightened her too. And they were always empty, even of ghosts. In these dreams, she ended up alone. From these dreams, she woke quietly, in the morning, with dried tears and an aching heart.

Still, she did not have the strength to tell him no.

When Tiberias Calore, heir to the throne of Norta, sank to a knee with a ring in hand, she took it. She smiled. She kissed him. She said yes.

"You have made me happier than I ever thought I could be," Tibe told her.

"I know the feeling," she replied, meaning every word. She was happy, yes, in her own way, as best she knew.

But there is a difference between a single candle in darkness, and a sunrise.

There was opposition among the High Houses. Queenstrial was their right, after all. To wed the most noble son to the most talented daughter.

House Merandus, Samos, Osanos were once the front-runners, their girls groomed to be queens only to have even the chance of a crown snatched away by some nobody. But the king stood firm. And there was precedent. At least two Calore kings before had wed outside the bonds of Queenstrial. Tibe would be the third.

As if to apologize for the Queenstrial slight, the rest of the wedding was rigidly traditional. They waited until Coriane turned sixteen the following spring, drawing out the engagement, allowing the royal family to convince, threaten, and buy their way to the acceptance of the High Houses. Eventually all agreed to the terms. Coriane Jacos would be queen but her children, all of them, would be subject to political weddings. A bargain she did not want to make, but Tibe was willing, and she could not tell him no.

Of course, Jessamine took credit for everything. Even as Coriane was laced into her wedding gown, an hour from marrying a prince, the old cousin crowed across a brimful glass. "Look at your bearing, those are Jacos bones. Slender, graceful, like a bird."

Coriane felt nothing of the sort. *If I was a bird, then I could fly away with Tibe.* The tiara on her head, the first of many, poked into her scalp. Not a good omen.

"It gets easier," Queen Anabel whispered into her ear. Coriane wanted to believe her.

With no mother of her own, Coriane had willingly accepted Anabel and Robert as substitute parents. In a perfect world, Robert would even walk her down the aisle instead of her father, who was still wretched. As a wedding gift, Harrus had asked for five thousand tetrarchs in allowance. He didn't seem to understand that presents were usually *given* to the bride, not requested of her. Despite her soon-to-be royal position, he had lost his governorship to poor management.

Already on thin ice due to Tibe's unorthodox engagement, the royals could do nothing to help and House Provos gleefully took up the governance of Aderonack.

After the ceremony, the banquet, and even after Tibe had fallen asleep in their new bedchamber, Coriane scrawled in her diary. The penmanship was hasty, slurred, with sloping letters and blots of ink that bled through the pages. She did not write often anymore.

I am married to a prince who will one day be a king. Usually this is where the fairy tale ends. Stories don't go much further than this moment, and I fear there's a good reason for it. A sense of dread hung over today, a black cloud I still can't be rid of. It is an unease deep in the heart of me, feeding off my strength. Or perhaps I am coming down with sickness. It's entirely possible. Sara will know.

I keep dreaming of her eyes. Elara's. Is it possible—could she be sending me these nightmares? Can whispers do such a thing? I must know. I must. I must. I MUST.

For her first act as a princess of Norta, Coriane employed a proper tutor, as well as taking Julian into her household. Both to hone her ability, and help her defend against what she called "annoyances." A carefully chosen word. Once more, she elected to keep her problems to herself, to stop her brother from worry, as well as her new husband.

Both were distracted. Julian by Sara, and Tibe by another well-guarded secret.

The king was sick.

It took two long years before the court knew anything was amiss.

"It's been like this for some time now," Robert said, one hand in Coriane's. She stood on a balcony with him, her face the picture of sorrow. The prince was still handsome, still smiling, but his vigor was gone, his skin gray and dark, leached of life. He seemed to be dying with the king. But Robert's was an ailment of the heart, not the bones and blood, as the healers said of the king's ills. A cancer, a gnawing, riddling Tiberias with rot and tumors.

He shivered, despite the sun above, not to mention the hot summer air. Coriane felt sweat on the back of her neck, but like Robert, she was cold inside.

"The skin healers can only do so much. If only he'd broken his spine, that'd be no trouble at all." Robert's laugh sounded hollow, a song without notes. The king was not yet dead, and already his consort was a shell of himself. And while she feared for her father-in-law, knowing that a painful, diseased death waited for him, she was terrified of losing Robert as well. *He cannot succumb to this. I won't let him.*

"It's fine, no need to explain," Coriane muttered. She did her best not to cry, though every inch of her hoped to. *How can this be happening? Are we not Silvers? Are we not gods?* "Does he need anything? Do you?"

Robert smiled an empty smile. His eyes flashed to her stomach, not yet rounded by the life inside. A prince or princess, she did not know yet. "He would have liked to have seen that one."

House Skonos tried everything, even cycling the king's blood. But whatever sickness he had never disappeared. It wasted at him faster than they could heal. Usually Robert stayed by him in his chamber, but today he left Tiberias alone with his son, and Coriane knew why. The end was near. The crown would pass, and there were things only Tibe could know.

The day the king died, Coriane marked the date and colored the entire diary page in black ink. She did the same a few months later, for Robert. His will was gone, his heart refusing to beat. Something ate at him too, and in the end, it swallowed him whole. Nothing could be done. No one could hold him back from taking shadowed flight.

Coriane wept bitterly as she inked the day of his ending in her diary.

She carried on the tradition. Black pages for black deaths. One for Jessamine, her body simply too old to continue. One for her father, who found his end in the bottom of a glass.

And three for the miscarriages she suffered over the years. Each one came at night, on the heels of a violent nightmare.

Coriane was twenty-one, and pregnant for a fourth time.

She told no one, not even Tibe. She did not want the heartache for him. Most of all, she wanted no one to know. If Elara Merandus was truly still plaguing her, turning her own body against her unborn children, she didn't want any kind of announcement regarding another royal child.

The fears of a fragile queen were no basis for banishing a High House, let alone one as powerful as Merandus. So Elara was still at court, the last of the three Queenstrial favorites still unmarried. She made no overtures to Tibe. On the contrary, she regularly petitioned to join Coriane's ladies, and was regularly denied her request.

It will be a surprise when I seek her out, Coriane thought, reviewing her meager but necessary plan. *She'll be off guard, startled enough for me to work.* She had practiced on Julian, Sara, even Tibe. Her abilities were better than ever. *I will succeed.*

The Parting Ball signaling the end of the season at the summer palace was the perfect cover. So many guests, so many minds. Elara would be easy to get close to. She would not expect Queen Coriane to speak to her, let alone *sing* to her. But Coriane would do both.

She made sure to dress for the occasion. Even now, with the wealth of the crown behind her, she felt out of place in her crimson and gold silks, a girl playing dress-up against the lords and ladies around her. Tibe whistled as he always did, calling her beautiful, assuring her she was the only woman for him—in this world or any other. Normally it calmed her, but now she was only nervous, focused on the task at hand.

Everything moved both too slowly and too quickly for her taste. The meal, the dancing, greeting so many curled smiles and narrowed eyes. She was still the Singer Queen to so many, a woman who bewitched her way to the throne. *If only that were true. If only I was what they thought me to be, then Elara would be of no consequence, I would not spend every night awake, afraid to sleep, afraid to dream.*

Her opportunity came deep into the night, when the wine was running low and Tibe was in his precious whiskey. She swept away from his side, leaving Julian to attend to her drunken king. Even Sara did not notice her queen steal away, to cross the path of Elara Merandus as she idled by the balcony doors.

"Come outside with me, won't you, Lady Elara?" Coriane said, her eyes wide and laser-focused on Elara's own. To anyone who might pass by, her voice sounded like music and a choir both, elegant, heartbreaking, dangerous. A weapon as devastating as her husband's flame.

Elara's eyes did not waver, locked upon Coriane's, and the queen felt her heart flutter. *Focus,* she told herself. *Focus, damn you.* If the Merandus woman could not be charmed, then Coriane would be in for something worse than her nightmares.

But slowly, sluggishly, Elara took a step back, never breaking eye contact. "Yes," she said dully, pushing the balcony door open with one hand.

They stepped out together, Coriane holding Elara by the shoulder, keeping her from wavering. Outside, the night was sticky hot, the last gasps of summer in the upper river valley. Coriane felt none of it. Elara's eyes were the only things in her mind.

"Have you been playing with my mind?" she asked, cutting directly to her intentions.

"Not for a while," Elara replied, her eyes faraway.

"When was the last time?"

"Your wedding day."

Coriane blinked, startled. *So long ago.* "What? What did you do?"

"I made you trip." A dreamy smile crossed Elara's features. "I made you trip on your dress."

"That—that's it?"

"Yes."

"And the dreams? The nightmares?"

Elara said nothing. *Because there's nothing for her to say,* Coriane knew. She sucked in a breath, fighting the urge to cry. *These fears are my own. They always have been. They always will be. I was wrong before I came to court, and I'm still wrong long after.*

"Go back inside," she finally hissed. "Remember none of this." Then she turned away, breaking the eye contact she so desperately needed to keep Elara under her control.

Like a person waking up, Elara blinked rapidly. She cast a single confused glance at the queen before hurrying away, back into the party.

Coriane moved in the opposite direction, toward the stone bannister ringing the balcony. She leaned over it, trying to catch her breath, trying not to scream. Greenery stretched below her, a garden of fountains and stone more than forty feet down. For a single, paralyzing second, she fought the urge to jump.

The next day, she took a guard into her service, to defend her from any Silver ability someone might use against her. If not Elara, than surely someone else of House Merandus. Coriane simply could not believe how her mind seemed to spin out of control, happy one second and then distraught the next, bouncing between emotions like a kite in a gale.

The guard was of House Arven, the silent house. His name was Rane, a savior clad in white, and he swore to defend his queen against all forces.

They named the baby Tiberias, as was custom. Coriane didn't care for the name, but acquiesced at Tibe's request, and his assurance that they would name the next after Julian. He was a fat baby, smiling early, laughing often, growing bigger by leaps and bounds. She nicknamed him Cal to distinguish him from his father and grandfather. It stuck.

The boy was the sun in Coriane's sky. On hard days, he split the darkness. On good days, he lit the world. When Tibe went away to the front, for weeks at a time now that the war ran hot again, Cal kept her safe. Only a few months old and better than any shield in the kingdom.

Julian doted on the boy, bringing him toys, reading to him. Cal was apt to break things apart and jam them back together incorrectly, to Coriane's delight. She spent long hours piecing his smashed gifts back together, amusing him as well as herself.

"He'll be bigger than his father," Sara said. Not only was she Coriane's chief lady-in-waiting, she was also her physician. "He's a strong boy."

While any mother would revel in those words, Coriane feared them. *Bigger than his father, a strong boy.* She knew what that meant for a Calore prince, an heir to the Burning Crown.

He will not be a soldier, she wrote in her newest diary. *I owe him that much. Too long the sons and daughters of House Calore have been fighting, too long has this country had a warrior king. Too long have we been at war, on the front and—and also within. It might be a crime to write such things, but I am a queen. I am the queen. I can say and write what I think.*

As the months passed, Coriane thought more and more of her childhood home. The estate was gone, demolished by the Provos governors, emptied of her memories and ghosts. It was too close to the Lakelander border for proper Silvers to live, even though the fighting was contained to the bombed-out territories of the Choke. Even though few Silvers died, despite the Reds dying by the thousands. Conscripted from every corner of the kingdom, forced to serve and fight. *My kingdom,* Coriane knew. *My husband signs every conscription renewal, never stopping the cycle, only complaining about the cramp in his hand.*

She watched her son on the floor, smiling with a single tooth, bashing a pair of wooden blocks together. *He will not be the same,* she told herself.

The nightmares returned in earnest. This time they were of her baby grown, wearing armor, leading soldiers, sending them into a curtain of smoke. He followed and never returned.

With dark circles beneath her eyes, she wrote what would become the second-to-last entry into her diary. The words seemed to be carved into the page. She had not slept in three days, unable to face another dream of her son dying.

The Calores are children of fire, as strong and destructive as their flame, but Cal will not be like the others before. Fire can destroy, fire can kill, but it can also create. Forest burned in the summer will be green by spring, better and stronger than before. Cal's flame will build and bring roots from the ashes of war. The guns will quiet, the smoke will clear, and the soldiers, Red and Silver both, will come home. One hundred years of war, and my son will bring peace. He will not die fighting. He will not. HE WILL NOT.

Tibe was gone, at Fort Patriot in Harbor Bay. But Arven stood just outside her door, his presence forming a bubble of relief. *Nothing can touch me while he is here,* she thought, smoothing the downy hair on Cal's head. *The only person in my head is me.*

The nurse who came to collect the baby noticed the queen's agitated manner, her twitching hands, the glazed eyes, but said nothing. It was not her place.

Another night came and went. No sleep, but one last entry in Coriane's diary. She had drawn flowers around each word—magnolia blossoms.

The only person in my head is me.

Tibe is not the same. The crown has changed him, as you feared it would. The fire is in him, the fire that will burn all the world. And it is in your son, in the prince who will never change his blood and will never sit a throne.

The only person in my head is me.

The only person who has not changed is you. You are still the little girl in a dusty room, forgotten, unwanted, out of place. You are queen of everything, mother to a beautiful son, wife to a king who loves you, and still you cannot find it in yourself to smile.

Still you make nothing.

Still you are empty.

The only person in your head is you.

And she is no one of any importance.

She is nothing.

The next morning, a maid found her bridal crown broken on the floor, an explosion of pearls and twisted gold. There was silver on it, blood dark from the passing hours.

And her bathwater was black with it.

The diary ended unfinished, unseen by any who deserved to read it.

Only Elara saw its pages, and the slow unraveling of the woman inside.

She destroyed the book like she destroyed Coriane.

And she dreamed of nothing.

STEEL SCARS

THE FOLLOWING MESSAGE HAS BEEN DECODED
CONFIDENTIAL, COMMAND CLEARANCE REQUIRED

Day 61 of Operation LAKER, Stage 3.
Operative: Colonel REDACTED.
Designation: RAM.
Origin: Solmary, LL.
Destination: COMMAND at REDACTED.

-Operation LAKER completed ahead of schedule, deemed successful.
Canals and lock points of LAKES PERIUS, MISKIN, and NERON under
control of the Scarlet Guard.
-Operatives WHIPPER and OPTIC will control LAKER moving forward,
maintain close contact, open channels to MOBILE BASE and COMMAND.
Stand-and-report protocol, awaiting action orders.
-Returning to TRIAL with LAMB at present.

-LAKER overview: Killed in action: D. FERRON, T. MILLS, M. PERCHER (3).

Wounded: SWIFTY, WISHBONE (2).

Silver casualty count (3): Greenwarden (1), Strongarm (1), Skin healer? (1).

Civilian casualty count: Unknown.

RISE, RED AS THE DAWN.

"Storms ahead."

The Colonel speaks to fill the silence. His one good eye presses to a crack in the compartment wall, fixing on the horizon. The other eye stares, though it can hardly see through a film of scarlet blood. Nothing new. His left eye has been like that for years.

I follow his gaze, peering through slats in the rattling wood. Dark clouds gather a few miles off, trying to hide behind the forested hills. In the distance, thunder rolls. I pay it no mind. I only hope the storms don't slow the train down, forcing us to spend one second longer hidden here, beneath the false floor of a cargo car.

We don't have time for thunderstorms or pointless conversation. I haven't slept in two days and I have the face to prove it. I want nothing more than quiet and a few hours of rest before we make it back to the base in Trial. Luckily there's not much to do here but lie down. I'm too tall to stand in such a space, as is the Colonel. We both have to sprawl, leaning as best we can in the dim partition. It'll be night soon, with only darkness to keep us company.

I can't complain about the mode of transportation. On the trip out to Solmary, we spent half the journey on a barge shipping fruit. It stalled out on Lake Neron, and most of the cargo rotted. Spent the first week of operations washing the stink from my clothes. And I'll never forget the mess before we started Laker, in Detraon. Three days in a cattle car, only to find the Lakelander capital utterly beyond reach. Too close to the Choke and the warfront to have shoddy defenses, a truth I willingly overlooked. But I wasn't an officer then, and it wasn't my decision to try to infiltrate a Silver capital without adequate intelligence or support. That was the Colonel. Back then he was only a captain with the code name Ram and too much to prove, too much to fight for. I only tagged along, barely more than an oathed soldier. I had things to prove too.

He continues to squint at the landscape. Not to look outside, but to avoid looking at me. *Fine.* I don't like looking at him either.

Bad blood or not, we make a good team. Command knows it, we know it, and that's why we keep getting sent out together. Detraon was our only misstep in an endless march for the cause. And for them, for the Scarlet Guard, we put aside our differences each and every time.

"Any idea where we go next?" Like the Colonel, I won't abide the heavy silence.

He pulls back from the wall, frowning, still not looking my way. "You know that's not how it works."

I've spent two years as an officer, two more as an oathed soldier of the Guard, and a lifetime living in its shadow. *Of course I know how it works,* I want to spit.

No one knows more than they must. No one is told anything beyond their operation, their squadron, their immediate superiors. Information is more dangerous than any weapon we possess. We learned that early, after decades of failed uprisings, all laid low by one captured Red in the hands of a Silver whisper. Even the best-trained soldier cannot resist an assault of the mind. They are always unraveled, their secrets always discovered. So my operatives and my soldiers answer to me, their captain. I answer to the Colonel, and he answers to Command, whoever they might be. We know only what we must to move forward. It's the only reason the Guard has lasted this long, surviving where no other underground organization has before.

But no system is perfect.

"Just because you haven't received new orders doesn't mean you don't have an *idea* as to what they might be," I say.

A muscle in his cheek twitches. To pull a frown or a smile, I don't know. But I doubt it's the latter. The Colonel doesn't smile, not truly. Not for many years.

"I have my suspicions," he replies after a long moment.

"And they are . . . ?"

"My own."

I hiss through my teeth. *Typical.* And probably for the best, if I'm being honest with myself. I've had enough close shaves of my own with Silver hunting dogs to know exactly how vital the Guard's secrecy is. My mind alone contains names, dates, operations, enough information to cripple the last two years of work in the Lakelands.

"Captain Farley."

We don't use our titles or names in official correspondence. I'm Lamb, according to anything that could be intercepted. Another defense. If any of our messages fall into the wrong hands, if the Silvers crack our cyphers, they'll have a hard time tracking us down and unraveling our vast, dedicated network.

"Colonel," I respond, and he finally looks at me.

Regret flashes in his one good eye, still a familiar shade of blue. The rest of him has changed over the years. He's noticeably harder, a wiry mass of old muscle, coiled like a snake beneath threadbare clothes. His blond hair, lighter than mine, has begun to thin. There's white at the temples. I can't believe I never noticed it before. He's getting old. But not slow. Not stupid. The Colonel is just as sharp and dangerous as ever.

I keep still under his quiet, quick observation. Everything is a test with him. When he opens his mouth, I know I've passed.

"What do you know about Norta?"

I grin harshly. "So they've finally decided to expand out."

"I asked you a question, Little Lamb."

The nickname is laughable. I'm almost six feet tall.

"Another monarchy like the Lakelands," I spit out. "Reds must work or conscript. They center on the coast, their capital is Archeon. At war with the Lakelands for nearly a century. They have an alliance with Piedmont. Their king is Tiberias—Tiberias the—"

"The Sixth," he offers. Chiding as a schoolteacher, not that I spent much time in school. His fault. "Of the House Calore."

Stupid. They don't even have brains enough to give their children different names.

"Burners," I add. "They lay claim to the so-called Burning Crown. Fitting opposite to the nymph kings of the Lakelands." A monarchy I know all too well, from a lifetime living beneath their rule. They are as unending and unyielding as the waters of their kingdom.

"Indeed. Opposite but also horribly alike."

"Then they should be just as easy to infiltrate."

He raises an eyebrow, gesturing to the cramped space around us. He almost looks amused. "You call this easy?"

"I haven't been shot at today, so, yes, I'd say so," I reply. "Besides, Norta is what, half the size of the Lakelands?"

"With comparable populations. Dense cities, a more advanced basis of infrastructure—"

"All the better for us. Crowds are easy to hide in."

He grits his teeth, annoyed. "Do you have an answer to every-thing?"

"I'm good at what I do."

Outside, the thunder rumbles again, closer than before.

"So we go to Norta next. Do what we've done here," I press on. Already, my body buzzes with anticipation. This is what I've been waiting for. The Lakelands are only one spoke of the wheel, one nation in a continent of many. A rebellion contained to its borders would eventually fail, stamped out by the other nations of the continent. But something bigger, a wave across two kingdoms, another foundation to explode beneath the Silvers' cursed feet—that has a chance. And a chance is all I require to do what I must.

The illegal gun at my hip has never felt so comforting.

"You must not forget, Captain." Now he's staring. I wish he wouldn't. *He looks so much like her.* "Where our skills truly lie. What we started as, what we came from."

Without warning, I slam my heel against the boards below us. He doesn't flinch. My anger is not a surprise.

"How could I forget?" I sneer. I resist the urge to tug at the long blond braid over my shoulder. "My mirror reminds me every day."

I never win arguments with the Colonel. But this feels like a draw at least.

He looks away, back to the wall. The last bit of sunlight glints through, illuminating the blood of his wounded eye. It glows red in the dying light.

His sigh is heavy with memory. "So does mine."

THE FOLLOWING MESSAGE HAS BEEN DECODED
CONFIDENTIAL, COMMAND CLEARANCE REQUIRED

Operative: Colonel REDACTED.
Designation: RAM.
Origin: Trial, LL.
Destination: COMMAND at REDACTED.

-Returned to TRIAL with LAMB.
-Reports of LL Silver pushback in ADELA verified.
-Request permission to dispatch HOLIDAY and her team to observe/
respond.
-Request permission to begin assessment of contact viability in NRT.

RISE, RED AS THE DAWN.

THE FOLLOWING MESSAGE HAS BEEN DECODED
CONFIDENTIAL, SENIOR CLEARANCE REQUIRED

Operative: General REDACTED.
Designation: DRUMMER.
Origin: REDACTED.
Destination: RAM at Trial, LL.

-Permission to dispatch HOLIDAY granted. Observe only, EYES ON
Operation.
-Permission to assess contact viability in NRT granted.
-LAMB will take point on Operation RED WEB, making contact with

smuggling and underground networks in NRT, emphasis on the WHISTLE black market ring. Orders enclosed, her eyes only. Must dispatch to NRT within week.

-RAM will take point on Operation SHIELDWALL. Orders enclosed, your eyes only. Must dispatch to Ronto within week.

RISE, RED AS THE DAWN.

Trial is the single largest city on the Lakelander border, its intricately carved walls and towers looking across Lake Redbone and deep into the heart of the Nortan backcountry. The lake hides a flooded city, all raided and stripped by nymph divers. Meanwhile, the slave workers of the Lakelands built Trial on the shores, in mockery of the drowned ruins and the Nortan wilderness.

I used to wonder what kinds of idiots are fighting this Silver war, if they insist on containing the battlegrounds to the forsaken Choke. The northern border is long and winding, cutting along the river, mostly forested on both sides, always defended but never attacked. Of course, in the winter, it's a brutal land of cold and snow, but what about the late spring and summer? *Now?* If Norta and the Lakelands hadn't been fighting for a century, I would expect an assault on the city at any moment. But there's nothing at all, and never will be.

Because the war is not a war at all.

It is an extermination.

Red soldiers conscript, fight, and die in the thousands, year after year. They're told to fight for their kings, to defend their country, their families, who would surely be overrun and overthrown if not for their forced bravery. And the Silvers sit back, moving their toy legions to and fro, trading blows that never seem to do much of anything. Reds are too small, too restricted, too uneducated to notice. It's sickening.

Only one of a thousand reasons I believe in the cause and in the Scarlet Guard. But belief doesn't make it easy to take a bullet. Not like the last time I returned to Irabelle, bleeding from the abdomen, unable to walk without the damned Colonel's aid. At least then I got a week to rest and heal. Now I doubt I'll be here much longer than a few days before they send us back out again.

Irabelle is the only proper Guard base in the region, to my limited knowledge at least. Safe houses scatter along the river and deeper into the woods, but Irabelle is certainly the beating heart of our organization. Partly underground and entirely overlooked, most of us would call Irabelle home if we had to. But most of us have no true home to speak of, none but the Guard and the Reds alongside us.

The structure is much larger than we need, easy for an outsider—or an invader—to get lost in. Perfect for seeking quiet. Not to mention most of the entrances and halls are rigged with floodgates. One order from the Colonel and the whole place goes under, drowned like the old world before it. It makes the place damp and cool in summer, frigid in winter, with walls like sheets of ice. No matter the season, I like to walk the tunnels, taking a lonely patrol through dim concrete passages forgotten by anyone but me. After my time on the train, avoiding the Colonel's accusing, crimson gaze, the cool air and open tunnel before me feels like the closet brush of freedom I'll ever know.

My gun spins idly on my finger, a careful balance I'm good at keeping. It's not loaded. I'm not stupid. But the lethal weight of it is still pleasing. *Norta.* The pistol keeps spinning. *Their arms laws are stricter than the Lakelands. Only registered hunters are allowed to carry. And those are few.* Just another obstacle I'm eager to overcome. I've never been to Norta, but I assume it's the same as the Lakelands. Just as Silver, just as dangerous, just as *ignorant*. A thousand executioners, a million to the noose.

I've long stopped questioning *why* this is allowed to continue. I was not raised to accept a master's cage, not like so, so many are. What I see as a maddening surrender is the only survival to so many others. I suppose I have the Colonel to thank for my stubborn belief in freedom. He never let me think otherwise. He never let me accept what we came from. Not that I'll ever tell him that. He's done too much to ever earn my thanks.

But so have I. That's fair, I suppose. And don't I believe in fairness?

Footsteps turn my head, and I slip the gun to my side, careful to keep it hidden. A fellow Guardsman would not mind the weapon, but a Silver officer certainly would. Not that I expect one to find us down here. They never do.

Indy doesn't bother with a greeting. She halts a few feet away, her tattoos evident against her tan skin even in the meager light. Thorns up one side, from her wrist to the crown of her shaved head, with roses winding down the other arm. Her code name is Holiday, but Garden would've been more fitting. She's a fellow captain, another one of us who answers to the Colonel. There's ten in all under his command, each with a larger detachment of oathed soldiers sworn to their captains.

"The Colonel wants you in his office. New orders," she says. Then her voice lowers, even though no one can hear us this deep into Irabelle. "He isn't happy."

I grin and push past her. She's shorter than me, like most people, and has to work to keep up. "Is he ever?"

"You know what I mean. This is different."

Her dark eyes flash, betraying a rare fear. I saw it last in the infirmary, as she stood over the body of another captain. Saraline, code named Mercy, who ended up losing a kidney during a routine arms raid. She's still recovering. The surgeon was shaky at best. *Not your fault. Not your job*, I remind myself. But I did what I could. I'm no stranger to blood and I was the best medic we had at the moment. Still, it was the first time I held a human organ in my hand. *At least she's alive.*

"She's walking," Indy offers, reading the guilt on my face. "Slow, but she's doing it."

"That's good," I say, neglecting to add that she should've been walking weeks ago. *Not your fault* echoes again.

When we make it back to the central hub, Indy breaks off, heading to the infirmary. She hasn't left Saraline's side for anything but assignments and, apparently, the Colonel's errands. They came to the Guard at the same time, close as sisters. And then, quite obviously, *not* sisters anymore. No one minds. There's no rules against fraternizing within the organization, so long as the job gets done and everyone comes back alive. So far, no one at Irabelle has been foolish or sentimental enough to let something so petty as a feeling jeopardize our cause.

I leave Indy to her worries and head in the opposite direction, to where I know the Colonel waits.

His office would make a marvelous tomb. No windows, concrete walls, and a lamp that always seems to burn out at precisely the wrong moment. There are far better places in Irabelle for him to conduct business, but he likes the quiet and the closed space. He's tall enough, and the low ceiling makes him seem like a giant. Probably why he likes the room so much.

His head scrapes the ceiling when he stands to greet my entrance.

"New orders?" I ask, already knowing the answer. We've been here two days. I know better than to expect any kind of vacation, even after the grand success of Operation Laker. The central passages of three lakes, each one key to the inner Lakelands, now belong to us, and no one is the wiser. For what higher purpose, I don't know. That's for Command to worry about, not me.

The Colonel slides a folded paper across the table to me. Sealed edges. I have to snap it open with a finger. *Strange.* I've never received sealed orders before.

My eyes scan the page, widening with every passing word. Command orders. Straight from the top, past the Colonel, directly to me.

"These are—"

He holds up a hand, stopping me short. "Command says your eyes only." His voice is controlled, but I hear the anger anyway. "It's your operation."

I have to clench a fist to keep calm. *My own operation.* Blood pounds in my ears, pressed on by a rising heartbeat. My jaw clenches, grinding my teeth together so I don't smile. I look back at the orders again to make sure they're real. *Operation Red Web.*

After a moment, I realize something is missing.

"There's no mention of you, sir."

He raises the eyebrow of his bad eye. "Do you expect there to be? I'm not your *nanny*, Captain." He bristles. The mask of control threatens to slip and he busies himself with an already pristine desk, flicking away a piece of dust that doesn't exist.

I shrug off the insult. "Very well. I assume you have orders of your own."

"I do," he says quickly.

"Then a bit of a celebration is in order."

The Colonel all but sneers. "You want to celebrate being a poster girl? Or would you rather cheer a suicide mission?"

Now I really do smile. "I don't see it that way." Slowly, I fold the orders again and slip them into my jacket pocket. "Tonight, I drink to my first independent assignment. And tomorrow, I head to Norta."

"*Your eyes only,* Captain."

When I reach the door, I glare at him over my shoulder. "As if you didn't already know."

His silence is admission enough.

"Besides, I'll still be reporting to you, so you can pass on my relays to Command," I add. I can't help but goad him a little. He deserves it for the nanny comment. "What's that called? Oh yes. The middleman."

"Careful, Captain."

I nod my head, smiling as I wrench open the office door. "Always, sir."

Thankfully, he doesn't let another uncomfortable silence linger. "Your broadcast crew is waiting in your barracks. Best get on."

"I do hope I'm camera ready." I giggle falsely, pretending to preen.

He waves a hand, officially dismissing me from his sight. I go willingly, weaving through the halls of Irabelle with enthusiasm.

To my surprise, the excitement pulsing through me doesn't last long. I started out sprinting to the barracks, intending to hunt down my team of oathed soldiers and tell them the good news. But my pace soon slows, my delight giving way to reluctance. And fear.

There's a reason they call us Ram and Lamb, other than the obvious. I've never been sent anywhere without the Colonel to follow. He's always been there, a safety net I've never wanted, but one I've become far too familiar with. He's saved my life too many times to count. And he's certainly why I'm here instead of a frozen village, losing fingers to every winter and friends to every round of conscription. We don't see eye to eye on much, but we always get the job done, and we always stay alive. We succeed where others can't. We survive. Now I must do the same alone. Now I have to protect others, taking their lives—and deaths—onto my shoulders.

My pace halts, allowing me a few more moments to collect myself. The cool shadows are calming, inviting. I press up against the slick concrete wall, letting the cold seep through me. *I must be like the Colonel when I assemble my team. I am their captain, their commander, and I must be perfect. No room for mistakes and no hesitation. Forward at all costs. Rise, Red as the dawn.*

The Colonel may not be a good person, but he's a brilliant leader. That's always been enough. And now I'll do my best to be the same.

I think better of my plan. Let the rest idle a few minutes longer.

I enter my barracks on my own, chin raised. I don't know why I was chosen for this, why Command wants me to be the one to shout our words. But I'm sure there's a good reason. A young woman holding a flag is quite a striking figure—but also a puzzling one. Silvers might send men and women to die on the lines in equal measure, but a rebel group led by a woman is easier to underestimate. Just what Command wants. Or they simply prefer I'm the one eventually identified and executed, rather than one of their own.

The first crewman, a slumtown escapee judging by his tattooed neck, waves me to the camera already waiting. Another hands me a red scarf and a typed message, one that will not be heard for many months.

But when it is, when it rings out across Norta and the Lakelands, it will land with the strength of a hammer's fall.

I face the cameras alone, my face hidden, my words steel.

"Rise, Red as the dawn."

THE FOLLOWING MESSAGE HAS BEEN DECODED
CONFIDENTIAL, COMMAND CLEARANCE REQUIRED

Operative: Colonel REDACTED.
Designation: RAM.
Origin: Trial, LL.
Destination: COMMAND at REDACTED.

-EYES ON team led by HOLIDAY met opposition in ADELA.
-ADELA safe house destroyed.
-EYES ON overview: Killed in action: R. INDY, N. CAWRALL,
T. TREALLER, E. KEYNE (4).
Silver casualty count: Zero (0).
Civilian casualty count: Unknown.

RISE, RED AS THE DAWN.
THE FOLLOWING MESSAGE HAS BEEN DECODED
CONFIDENTIAL, SENIOR CLEARANCE REQUIRED

Day 4 of Operation RED WEB, Stage 1.
Operative: Captain REDACTED.
Designation: LAMB.
Origin: Harbor Bay, NRT.
Destination: RAM at REDACTED.

-Transit smooth through ADERONACK, GREATWOODS, MARSH COAST
regions.
-BEACON region transit difficult, heavy NRT military presence.
-Made contact with MARINERS. Entered HARBOR BAY with their aid.
-Meeting with EGAN, head of the MARINERS. Will assess.

RISE, RED AS THE DAWN.

* * *

As any good cook can tell you, there are always rats in the kitchen.

The Kingdom of Norta is no different. Its cracks and crevices crawl with what the Silver elite would call vermin. Red thieves, smugglers, army deserters, teenagers fleeing conscription, or feeble elders trying to escape punishment for the idle "crime" of growing old. In the backcountry, farther north toward the Lakeland border, they keep to the woods and small villages, finding safety in the places no self-respecting Silver would condescend to live. But in cities like Harbor Bay, where Silvers keep fine houses and ugly laws, Reds turn to more desperate measures. And so must I.

Boss Egan is not easy to get to. His so-called associates take me and my lieutenant, Tristan, through a maze of tunnels under the walls of the coastal city. We double back more than once, to confuse me as well as anyone who might try to follow. I all but expect Melody, the soft-voiced and sharped-eyed thief leading the way, to blindfold us. Instead, she lets the darkness do its work, and by the time we emerge, I can barely find true north, let alone my way out of the city.

Tristan is not a trusting man, having learned well at the hands of the Scarlet Guard. He hovers at my side, one hand inside his jacket, always gripping the long knife he keeps close. Melody and her men laugh off the obvious threat, pulling back coats and shawls to reveal edged weapons of their own.

"Not to worry, Stretch," she says, raising an eyebrow at Tristan's scraping height. "You're well protected."

He flushes, angry, but doesn't loosen his grasp. And I'm still keenly aware of the knife in my boot, not to mention the pistol tucked into the back of my pants.

Melody keeps walking, leading us through a market trembling with noise and the sharp smell of fish. Her thick body cuts through the crowd, which parts to let her pass. The tattoo on her upper arm, a blue anchor surrounded by red, coiling rope, is warning enough. She's a Mariner, a member of the smuggling operation Command assigned me to feel out. And judging by the way she orders her own detachment, three of them following her lead, she's highly ranked and well respected.

I feel her assessing me, even though her eyes are forward. For this reason, I decided not to take the rest of my team into the city to meet with her boss. Tristan and I are enough to evaluate his operation, judge his motives, and report back.

Egan, it seems, takes the opposite approach.

I expect a subterranean stronghold much like ours at Irabelle, but Melody leads us to an ancient lighthouse, its walls weathered by age and the salty air. Once a beacon used to guide ships into port; now it's too far from the water, as the city expanded out into the harbor. From the outside, it looks abandoned, its windows shuttered and doors barred. The Mariners pay it no mind. They don't even bother to hide their approach, though every instinct in me screams for discretion. Instead, Melody leads us across the open market, head high.

The crowd moves with us like a school of fish. Providing camouflage. Escorting us all the way to the lighthouse and a battered, locked door. I blink at the action, noting how well organized the Mariners seem to be. They command respect, that's obvious, not to mention loyalty. Both valuable prizes to the Scarlet Guard, things that cannot truly be bought with money or intimidation. My heart leaps in my chest. The Mariners look to be viable allies indeed.

Once safely inside the lighthouse, at the foot of an endless, spiraling stair, I feel a cord of tension release in my chest. I'm no stranger to infiltrating Silver cities, prowling the streets with poor intent, but I certainly don't enjoy it. Especially without the Colonel at my side, a gruff but effective shield against anything that might befall us.

"You're not afraid of officers?" I wonder aloud, watching as one of the Mariners locks the door behind us. "They don't know you're here?"

Again, Melody chuckles. She's already a dozen steps up, and still climbing. "Oh, they know we're here."

Tristan's eyes almost bug out of his head. "What?" He blanches, mirroring my thoughts.

"I said, Security knows we're here," she repeats. Her voice echoes.

When I put a foot on the first step, Tristan grabs my wrist. "We shouldn't be here, Cap—" he murmurs, forgetting himself. I don't give him the chance to say my name, to go against the rules and protocols that have protected us for so long. Instead I jam my forearm into his windpipe, pushing him back against stairs with all my strength. He sprawls, falling, his weedy length stretched across several steps.

My face flushes with heat. This isn't something I want to do, in front of outsiders or not. Tristan is a good lieutenant, if overprotective. I don't know what's more damaging—showing the Mariners dissension in our ranks or showing them fear. I hope it's the latter. With a calculated shrug, I step back and offer my hand to Tristan but no apology. He knows why.

And without another word, he follows me up the stairs.

Melody lets us pass and I feel her eyes with every step. She is certainly watching me now. And I let her, my face and manner impassive. I do my best to be like the Colonel, unreadable and unflinching.

At the crown of the lighthouse, the boarded-up windows give way to a wide view of Harbor Bay. Literally built on top of another ancient city, the Bay is an old knot. The narrow lanes and twists are better suited to horses rather than transports, and we had to duck into alleys to avoid being run over. From this vantage point, I can see everything centers around the famous harbor, with too many alleys, tunnels, and forgotten corners to fully patrol. Paired with a high concentration of Reds, Harbor Bay is a perfect place for the Scarlet Guard to start. Our intelligence identified the city as the most viable root of Red rebellion in Norta, when an uprising comes. Unlike the capital, Archeon, where the seat of government demands absolute command, Harbor Bay is not so controlled.

But it is not undefended. There's a military base built out on the water, dividing the perfect semicircle of land and waves in two. *Fort Patriot.* A hub for the Nortan army, navy, and air force, the only one of its kind to serve all three branches of the Silver military. Like the rest of the city, its walls and buildings are painted white, tipped with blue roofs and tall silver spires. I try to memorize it from this vantage point. Who knows when the knowledge might come in handy? And thanks to the useless war currently being fought in the north, Fort Patriot is entirely blind to the city around it. The soldiers keep to their walls, while Security keep the city in line. According to reports, they protect their own, the Silver citizens, but the Reds of the Bay largely govern themselves, with separate groups and bands keeping their own sort of order. Three in particular.

The Red Watch forms a police force of sorts, upholding what Red justice they can, protecting and enforcing laws Silver Security won't bother with. They settle Red disputes and crimes committed against our own, to prevent any more abuse by merciless, Silver-blooded hands. Their work is acknowledged, tolerated even by the officers of the city, and for this reason, I will not go to them. Noble as their cause might be, they run too close to Silvers for my taste.

But the Seaskulls, a glorified gang, make me just as wary. They are violent by all accounts, a trait I would normally admire. Their business is blood, and they have the feel of a rabid dog. Vicious, relentless, and stupid, their members are often executed and quickly replaced. They maintain control of their sector of the city through murder and blackmail, and often find themselves at odds with their rival operation, the Mariners.

Who I must assess for myself.

"You're Lamb, I presume."

I turn on my heel, away from the horizon stretching in all directions.

The man I assume to be Egan leans against the opposite windows, either unaware or unafraid of the fact that nothing but aged glass stands between him and a long fall. Like me, he's putting on a charade, showing the cards he wants while hiding the rest.

I came here with only Tristan to present a certain image. Egan, flanked by Melody and a troop of Mariners, elects to show his strength. To impress me. *Good.*

He crosses his arms, displaying two muscled and scarred forearms marked with twin anchor tattoos. I'm reminded of the Colonel, though they look nothing alike. Egan is short, squat, barrel-chested, with sun-damaged skin and long, salt-worn hair in a tangled plait. I don't doubt he's spent half his life on a boat.

"Or at least, that's whatever code name you've been saddled with," Egan continues, grinning. He's missing a good amount of teeth. "Am I right?"

I shrug, noncommittal. "Does my name matter?"

"Not at all. Only your intentions. And those are?"

Matching his grin, I cross to the center of the room, careful to avoid the sunken circle where the lighthouse lantern used to live. "I believe you know that already." My orders stated contact was made, but not to what extent. A necessary omission, to make sure outsiders cannot use our correspondence against us.

"Yes, well, I know well enough the goals and tactics of your people, but I'm talking to you. What are *you* here for?"

Your people. The words twinge, tugging at my brain. I'll decipher them later. I wish very much for a fistfight, instead of this nauseating game of back-and-forth. I'd rather a black eye than a puzzle.

"My goal is to establish open lines of communication. You're a smuggling operation, and having friends across the border is beneficial to us both." With another winning smile, I run my fingers through my braided hair. "I'm just a messenger, sir."

"Oh, I don't think I'd ever call a captain of the Scarlet Guard *just* a messenger."

This time, Tristan keeps still. It's my turn to react, despite my training. Egan doesn't miss my eyes widen or my cheeks flush. His deputies, Melody especially, have the audacity to smirk among themselves.

Your people. The Scarlet Guard. He's met us before.

"I'm not the first, then."

Another manic grin. "Not by a long shot. We've been running goods for yours since . . ." He glances at Melody, pausing for effect. "Two years ago, was it?"

"September 300, Boss," she replies.

"Ah, yes. I take it you don't know anything about that, Sheep."

I fight the urge to grit my teeth and growl. *Discretion*, the orders said. I doubt tossing one up-jumped criminal from his decaying tower is considered discreet. "It's not our way." And that's the only explanation I offer. Because while Egan thinks himself above me, far more informed than I am, he's wrong. He has no idea what we are, what we've done, and how much more we plan to do. He can't even fathom it.

"Well, your comrades pay well, that's for certain." He jingles a bracelet, nicely crafted silver, braided like rope. "I expect you'll do the same."

"If you do what's asked, yes."

"Then I'll do what's asked."

One nod at Tristan sets his wheels spinning. He tromps to my side in two long steps, so fast and gangly Egan laughs.

"Stars, you're a twiggy one," Egan says. "What do they call you? Beanpole?"

A corner of my mouth twitches, but I don't smile. For Tristan's sake. No matter how much he eats or trains, he can't seem to gain any sort of muscle. Not that it makes much difference where he's concerned. Tristan is a gunman, a sniper, not a brawler. He's most valuable a hundred yards away with a good rifle. I won't mention to Egan that his code name is Bones.

"We require overview and introduction to the so-called Whistle network," Tristan says, making my demands for me. Another tactic of the Colonel's that I've adopted. "We're looking for viable contacts in these key areas."

He passes over a marked map, plain but for the red dots on important cities and crossroads throughout the country. I know it without looking. The industrial slums of Gray Town and New Town; the capital, Archeon; Delphie; the military city Corvium; and many smaller towns and villages in between. Egan doesn't glance at the paper, but nods all the same, a picture of confidence.

"Anything else?" he gravels out.

Tristan glances my way, giving me one last chance to refuse this final order from Command. But I won't.

"We will require use of your smuggling network soon."

"Easy enough. With the Whistles, the whole country's open to you. You can send lightbulbs from here to Corvium and back if you want."

I can't help but smile, showing my teeth.

But Egan's grin fades a little. He knows there's more. "What's the cargo?"

With quick hands, I drop a tiny bag of tetrarch coins at his feet. All silver. Enough to convince him.

"The right people."

THE FOLLOWING MESSAGE HAS BEEN DECODED
CONFIDENTIAL, SENIOR CLEARANCE REQUIRED

Day 6 of Operation RED WEB, Stage 1.
Operative: Captain REDACTED.
Designation: LAMB.
Origin: Harbor Bay, NRT.
Destination: RAM at REDACTED.

-MARINERS led by EGAN agree to terms. Will run BEACON region
transport upon undertaking of RED WEB Stage 2.
-Be advised, MARINERS aware of SG organization. Other cells active in
NRT. Request clarification?

RISE, RED AS THE DAWN.

THE FOLLOWING MESSAGE HAS BEEN DECODED
CONFIDENTIAL, SENIOR CLEARANCE REQUIRED

Operative: Colonel REDACTED.
Designation: RAM.
Origin: REDACTED.
Destination: LAMB at Harbor Bay, NRT.

-Disregard. Focus on RED WEB.

RISE, RED AS THE DAWN.

THE FOLLOWING MESSAGE HAS BEEN DECODED
CONFIDENTIAL, SENIOR CLEARANCE REQUIRED

Day 10 of Operation RED WEB, Stage 1.
Operative: Captain REDACTED.
Designation: LAMB.
Origin: Albanus, NRT.
Destination: RAM at REDACTED.

-Made contacts in WHISTLE network across BEACON region/into
CAPITAL VALLEY, all Stage 2 willing.
-Working way up the CAPITAL RIVER.
-Town of ALBANUS closest Red center to SUMMERTON (seasonal home
of King Tiberias + his govt).
-Valuable? Will assess.

RISE, RED AS THE DAWN.

The locals call it the Stilts. I can see why. The river is still high, flooded
by the spring melts, and much of the town would be underwater if not

for the high pylons its structures are built on. An arena frowns over it all from the crest of a hill. A firm reminder of who owns this place and who rules this kingdom.

Unlike the larger cities of Harbor Bay or Haven, there are no walls, no gates, and no blood checks. My soldiers and I enter in the morning with the rest of the merchants moving along the Royal Road. A Silver officer checks our false identification cards with a disinterested flicker of a glance before waving us on, letting a pack of wolves into his village of sheep. If not for the location and Albanus's proximity to the king's summer palace, I wouldn't give this place another glance. There's nothing here of use. Just overworked woodcutters and their families, barely alive enough to eat, let alone rebel against a Silver regime. But Summerton is a few miles upriver, making Albanus worthy of my attention.

Tristan memorized the town before we entered, or at least he tried to. It would not do to consult our maps openly and let everyone know we do not belong. He turns left quickly. The rest of us follow, tracking off the paved Royal Road to the muddy, rutted avenue that runs along the swollen riverbank. Our boots sink, but no one slips.

The stilt houses rise on the left, dotting what I think is Marcher Road. A few dirty children watch us pass, idly throwing stones in the lapping river. Farther out, fishermen on their boats haul glistening nets, filling their little boats with the day's catch. They laugh among themselves, happy to work. Happy to have jobs that keep them from conscription and pointless war.

The Whistle in Orienpratis, a quarry city on the edge of the Beacon, is the reason we're here. She assured us that another one of her kind operated in Albanus, serving as a fence for the town's thieves and not-so-legal dealings. But she told us only that a Whistle existed, not where to find him or her. Not because she didn't trust me but because she didn't know who operated in Albanus. Like in the Scarlet Guard, the Whistles use their own secrets as a shield. So I keep my eyes open and searching.

The Stilts market throbs with activity. It's going to rain soon, and everyone wants to finish their errands before the downpour. I brush my braid over my left shoulder. A signal. Without looking, I know my Guardsmen split off, moving in the usual pairs. Their orders are clear. Case the market. Feel out potential leads. Find the Whistle if you can. With their packs of harmless contraband—glass beads, batteries, stale ground coffee—they'll attempt to trade or sell their way to the fence. *So will I.* My own pouch dangles at my hip, heavy but small, hidden by the untucked hem of a rough cotton shirt. Inside are bullets. Mismatched, of different calibers, seemingly stolen. In fact, they came from our own cache at our new Nortan safe house, a glorified cave tucked away in the Greatwoods region. But no one in the town can know that.

As always, Tristan keeps close. But he's more relaxed here. Smaller towns and villages are not dangerous, not by our standards. Even though Silver Security officers patrol the market, they are few, and uninterested. They don't care much if Reds steal from each other. Their punishments are reserved for the bold, the ones who dare look a Silver in the eye, or make enough trouble they have to get off their asses and involve.

"I'm hungry," I say, turning to a stall selling coarse bread. The prices are astronomical compared to what we're used to in the Lakelands, but then, Norta is no good at growing grain. Their soil is too rocky for much success in farming. How this man supports himself selling bread no one can buy is a mystery. Or it would be, to someone else.

The bread baker, a man too slim for his occupation, barely glances at us. We don't look like promising customers. I jingle the coins in my pocket to get his attention.

He finally looks up, eyes watery and wide. The sound of coinage this far from the cities surprises him. "What you see is what I have."

No nonsense. I like him already. "These two," I reply, pointing to the finest baked loaves he has. Not a very high bar.

Still, his eyebrows raise. He snaps up the bread, wrapping the loaves in old paper with practiced efficiency. When I produce the copper coins without haggling for a lower price, his surprise deepens. As does his suspicion.

"I don't know you," he mutters. He glances away, far to the right, where an officer busies himself berating several underfed children.

"We're traders," Tristan offers. He leans forward, bracing himself on the rickety frame of the bread stall. One sleeve lifts, showing something on his wrist. A red band circling all the way around, the mark of the Whistles as we've come to find. It's a tattoo, and a false one. *But the baker doesn't know that.*

The man's eyes linger on Tristan for only a moment, before trailing back to me. Not so foolish as he looks, then. "And what are you looking to trade?" he says, pushing one of the loaves into my hands. The other he keeps. Waiting.

"This and that," I reply. And then I whistle, soft and low, but unmistakable. The two-note tune the last Whistle taught me. Harmless to those who know nothing.

The baker does not smile or nod. His face betrays nothing. "You'll find better business in the dark."

"I always do."

"Down Mill Road, around the bend. A wagon," the baker adds. "After sunset, but before midnight."

Tristan nods. He knows the place.

I dip my head as well, in a tiny gesture of thanks. The baker doesn't offer his own. Instead, his fingers curl around my other loaf of bread, which he puts back down on the stall counter. In a single motion, he tears off its paper wrappings and takes a taunting bite. Crumbs flake into his meager beard, each one a message. My coin has been traded for something more valuable than bread.

Mill Road, around the bend.

Fighting a smile, I pull my braid over my right shoulder.

All over the market, my soldiers abandon their pursuits. They move as one, a school of fish following their leader. As we make our way back out of the market, I try to ignore the grumblings of two Guardsmen. Apparently, someone picked their pockets.

"All those batteries, gone in a second. Didn't even notice," Cara grumbles, pawing through her satchel.

I glance at her. "Your comm?" If her broadcaster, a tiny radio that passes our messages in beeps and clicks, is gone, we'll be in serious trouble.

Thankfully, she shakes her head and pats a bump in her shirt. "Still here," she says. I force a simple nod, swallowing my sigh of relief.

"Hey, I'm missing some coin!" another Guardsman, the muscle-bound Tye, mutters. She shoves her scarred hands into her pockets.

This time, I almost laugh. We entered the market looking for a master thief, and my soldiers fell prey to a pickpocket instead. On another day, I might be angry, but the tiny hiccup rolls right off my shoulders. A few lost coins are of no matter in the scheme of things. After all, the Colonel called our endeavor a suicide mission only a few weeks ago.

But we are succeeding. And we are still very much alive.

THE FOLLOWING MESSAGE HAS BEEN DECODED
CONFIDENTIAL, SENIOR CLEARANCE REQUIRED

Day 11 of Operation RED WEB, Stage 1.
Operative: Captain REDACTED.
Designation: LAMB.
Origin: Albanus, NRT.
Destination: RAM at REDACTED.

-ALBANUS/STILTS WHISTLE willing to collaborate w/ Stage 2.
-Has eyes inside SUMMERTON/King's seasonal palace.
-Also mentioned contacts within the Red Army at CORVIUM. Will pursue.

RISE, RED AS THE DAWN.

THE FOLLOWING MESSAGE HAS BEEN DECODED
CONFIDENTIAL, SENIOR CLEARANCE REQUIRED

Operative: Colonel REDACTED.
Designation: RAM.
Origin: REDACTED.
Destination: LAMB at Albanus.

-Not orders, too dangerous. Continue with RED WEB.

RISE, RED AS THE DAWN.

THE FOLLOWING MESSAGE HAS BEEN DECODED
CONFIDENTIAL, SENIOR CLEARANCE REQUIRED

Day 12 of Operation RED WEB, Stage 1.
Operative: Captain REDACTED.
Designation: LAMB.
Origin: Siracas, NRT.
Destination: RAM at REDACTED.

-Intent of RED WEB Stage 1 is to introduce SG into NRT via existing networks. Army within orders.
-Red Army contacts invaluable. Will pursue. Pass up message to COMMAND.
-En route to CORVIUM.

RISE, RED AS THE DAWN.

THE FOLLOWING MESSAGE HAS BEEN DECODED
CONFIDENTIAL, SENIOR CLEARANCE REQUIRED

Operative: Colonel REDACTED.
Designation: RAM.
Origin: REDACTED.
Destination: LAMB at Siracas.

-Stand down. Do not proceed to CORVIUM.

RISE, RED AS THE DAWN.

THE FOLLOWING MESSAGE HAS BEEN DECODED
CONFIDENTIAL, SENIOR CLEARANCE REQUIRED

Operative: General REDACTED.

Designation: DRUMMER.

Origin: REDACTED.

Destination: LAMB at Siracas, RAM at REDACTED.

-Proceed to CORVIUM. Assess Red Army contacts for information and
Stage 2/Asset Removal.

RISE, RED AS THE DAWN.

THE FOLLOWING MESSAGE HAS BEEN DECODED
CONFIDENTIAL, COMMAND CLEARANCE REQUIRED

Day 12 of Operation RED WEB.

Operative: Captain REDACTED.

Designation: LAMB.

Origin: Corvium, NRT.

Destination: COMMAND at REDACTED, RAM at REDACTED.

-Acknowledged.

-Clearly not too dangerous.

RISE, RED AS THE DAWN.

THE FOLLOWING MESSAGE HAS BEEN DECODED
CONFIDENTIAL, COMMAND CLEARANCE REQUIRED

Operative: Colonel REDACTED.

Designation: RAM.

Origin: REDACTED.
Destination: COMMAND at REDACTED.

-Please note my strong opposition to developments in RED WEB. LAMB
needs a short leash.

RISE, RED AS THE DAWN.

THE FOLLOWING MESSAGE HAS BEEN DECODED
CONFIDENTIAL, SENIOR CLEARANCE REQUIRED

Operative: General REDACTED.
Designation: DRUMMER.
Origin: REDACTED.
Destination: RAM at REDACTED.

-Noted.

RISE, RED AS THE DAWN.

I can smell the Choke from here. Ash, smoke, corpses.

"It's a slow day. No bombs yet." Tye fixes her eyes on the northwest
horizon, and the dark haze in the distance that can only be the front of
this pointless war. She served on the lines herself, albeit on the opposite
side we are now. She fought for Lakelander masters and lost an ear to
a frostbitten winter in trenches. She doesn't hide the deformity. Her
blond hair is pulled back tightly, letting everyone see the ruined stump
her so-called loyalty bought her.

Tristan scans the landscape for the third time, squinting through the scope of his long rifle. He lies on his belly, half-hidden by the ropy spring grass. His motions are slow and methodical, practiced in the gun range at Irabelle, as well as the deep forests of the Lakelands. The notches on the barrel, tiny scratches in the metal, stand out brightly in the daylight. Twenty-two in all, one for every Silver killed with that very weapon. For all his itchy paranoia, Tristan has a surprisingly steady trigger finger.

From our place on the rise, we have a commanding view of the surrounding woods. The Choke some miles to the northwest, clouded even under the morning sun, and Corvium another mile to the east. There are no more towns here, or even animals. Too close to the trench lines for anything but soldiers. But they keep to the Iron Road, the main thoroughfare that passes through Corvium and ends at the front lines. Over the last few days, we've learned much about the Red legions constantly moving, replacing defeated soldiers on the lines, only to march back with their own dead and wounded a week later. They march in at dawn and late evening. We keep our distance from the Road, but we can still hear them when they go. Five thousand in each legion, five thousand of our Red brothers and sisters resigned to living targets. Supply convoys are harder to predict, moving when required, and not on any schedule. They too are manned by Red soldiers and Silver officers, albeit officers of the useless kind. There's no honor in commanding a transport full of stale food and worn bandages. The supply convoys are a punishment for Silvers, and a reprieve for Reds. And best of all, they are poorly guarded. After all, the Lakelander enemy is firmly on the other side of the Choke, separated by miles of wasteland, trenches, and popping artillery. No one looks to the trees as they pass. No one suspects another enemy already inside their diamondglass walls.

I can't see the Iron Road from this ridge—the trees are in full leaf, obscuring the paved avenue—but we're not watching the Road today. We aren't gathering intelligence from troop movements. We're going to talk to the troops themselves.

My internal clock tells me they are late.

"Could be a trap," Tristan mutters, always eager to voice his panicked opinion. He keeps his eye firmly pressed to the scope in warning. He's been expecting a trap since the moment Will Whistle told us about his army contacts. And now that we're going to meet them, he's been on edge more than usual, if that's possible. Not a bad instinct to have, but not a helpful one at the moment. Risk is part of the game. We won't get anywhere if we think only of our own skins.

But there is a reason only three of us are waiting,

"If it's a trap, we'll get out of it," I reply. "We've beaten worse."

It's not a lie. We all have scars and ghosts of our own. Some drove us to the Scarlet Guard, and some were because of it. I know the sting of both.

My words are for Tye more than Tristan. Like all who escaped the trenches, she's not at all happy to be back, even if she isn't wearing a Lakelander's blue uniform. Not that she would ever complain about this out loud. But I can tell.

"Movement."

Tye and I crouch lower, whipping in the direction of Tristan's gaze. The rifle nose tracks at a snail's pace, following something in the trees. Four shadows. *Outnumbered.*

They emerge with their palms out, showing empty hands. Unlike the soldiers on the Road, these four have their uniforms turned inside out, favoring stained brown and black lining over their usual rust colors. Better camouflage for the woods. Not to mention their names and ranks. I can't see any insignia or badges of any kind. I have no idea who they are.

A calm breeze rustles the grass. It ripples like a pond disturbed by a single stone, its green waves breaking against the four as they approach in single file. I narrow my eyes at their feet. They're careful to step in the leader's footprints. Any tracker would think only one person came this way, not four. *Smart*.

A woman leads, her jaw like an anvil. She's missing both her trigger fingers. Unable to shoot, but still a soldier, judging by the crags of weariness on her face. Like the willowy, copper-skinned girl on her heels, her head is shaved to the scalp.

Two men bring up the rear. They are young, both probably within their first year of conscription. Neither is scarred or visibly injured, so they can't be masquerading as wounded back in Corvium. Supply soldiers, most likely. Lucky to haul crates of ammunition and food. Although the second, the one at the very back, seems too slight for manual labor.

The bald woman stops ten feet away, her palms still raised. Too close for both our liking. I force myself to stand from the grass and close the distance between us. Tye and Tristan keep still, not hidden, but not moving either.

"We're the ones," she says.

I keep my hands on my hips, fingers inches from the gun belted across my waist. A naked threat. "Who sent us?" I ask her in testing. Behind me, Tristan tightens like a snake. The woman has the bravery to keep her eyes from his rifle, but the others behind her don't.

"Will Whistle of the Stilts," she replies. She doesn't stop there, though it's enough for the moment. "Children taken from their mothers, soldiers sent to slaughter, countless generations of slavery. Each and every one of them sent you."

My fingers drum quietly. Rage is a double-edged sword, and this woman has been bled by both edges. "The Whistle will do. And you are?"

"Corporal Eastree, of the Tower Legion, like the rest." She gestures behind, to the other three still watching Tristan. I nod at him, and his trigger finger relaxes a little. But not much. "We're support troops, conscripted to Corvium."

"Will told me as such," I lie quickly. "And what did he tell you of me?"

"Enough to get us out here. Enough to risk our necks for." The voice comes from the lean young man at the back of the line. He angles forward, around his comrade, his smile crooked, teasing, and cold. His eyes flash. "You know it's execution if we're caught out here, right?"

Another breeze, sharper than the last. I force my own empty grin. "Oh, is that all?"

"We best make this quick," Eastree says. "Your lot might protect your names, but we have no use for such things. They have our blood, our faces. This is Private Florins, Private Reese, and—"

The one with the crooked smile steps out of line before she can say his name. He crosses the gap between us, though he doesn't extend a hand to shake. "I'm Barrow. Shade Barrow. And you better not get me killed."

My eyes narrow at him. "No promises."

THE FOLLOWING MESSAGE HAS BEEN DECODED
CONFIDENTIAL, SENIOR CLEARANCE REQUIRED

Day 23 of Operation RED WEB, Stage 1.
Operative: Captain REDACTED.
Designation: LAMB.
Origin: Corvium, NRT.
Destination: RAM at REDACTED.

-CORVIUM intelligence enclosed: fort statistics, city map, tunnel overlay,
army schedules/timetables.
-Early assessment: Most promising are Corp E (eager, angry, a gamble)
and Aide B (connected, officer's aide recently stationed to CORVIUM).
Possible for recruitment or Stage 2.
-Both seem willing to pledge but are otherwise ignorant to SG presence
in NRT, LL. Invaluable to have two operatives inside CORVIUM. Will
continue progress, request to fast-track recruitment?

RISE, RED AS THE DAWN.

THE FOLLOWING MESSAGE HAS BEEN DECODED
CONFIDENTIAL, SENIOR CLEARANCE REQUIRED

Operative: Colonel REDACTED.
Designation: RAM.
Origin: REDACTED.
Destination: LAMB at Corvium.

-Request denied. Corp E and Aide B nonessential.

-Move on from CORVIUM. Continue assessing WHISTLE contacts/RED WEB Stage 2 assets.

RISE, RED AS THE DAWN.

THE FOLLOWING MESSAGE HAS BEEN DECODED
CONFIDENTIAL, SENIOR CLEARANCE REQUIRED

Operative: Captain REDACTED.
Designation: LAMB.
Origin: Corvium, NRT.
Destination: RAM at REDACTED.

-CORVIUM intelligence vital to SG cause at large. Request more time at location. Pass up to COMMAND.

-Firmly believe Corp E and Aide B are strong candidates.

RISE, RED AS THE DAWN.

THE FOLLOWING MESSAGE HAS BEEN DECODED
CONFIDENTIAL, SENIOR CLEARANCE REQUIRED

Operative: General REDACTED.
Designation: DRUMMER.
Origin: REDACTED.
Destination: LAMB at Corvium, RAM at REDACTED.

-Request denied. Orders are to continue Stage 1 assessment

for Stage 2/Asset Removal.

RISE, RED AS THE DAWN.

THE FOLLOWING MESSAGE HAS BEEN DECODED
CONFIDENTIAL, COMMAND CLEARANCE REQUIRED

Operative: Captain REDACTED.
Designation: LAMB.
Origin: Corvium, NRT.
Destination: DRUMMER at REDACTED.

-Strong opposition. Many military assets present at CORVIUM, must be
assessed for Stage 2 removal.
-Request more time at location.

RISE, RED AS THE DAWN.

THE FOLLOWING MESSAGE HAS BEEN DECODED
CONFIDENTIAL, SENIOR CLEARANCE REQUIRED

Operative: General REDACTED.
Designation: DRUMMER.
Origin: REDACTED.
Destination: LAMB at Corvium.

-Request denied. Move out.

RISE, RED AS THE DAWN.

Following protocol, I light the thin strip of correspondence paper on fire. The dots and dashes detailing Command orders char away to nothing, consumed by flame. I know the feeling. Hot anger licks at my insides. But I keep my face still, for Cara's sake.

She looks on, thick glasses perched on her nose. Her fingers itch, ready to click out my response to orders she cannot read.

"No need," I say, waving her off. The lie sits in my mouth for a moment. "Command bent. We stay."

I bet the Colonel's damned red eye is rolling in his skull right now. But his orders are stupid, narrow-minded, and now Command thinks the same. They must be disobeyed, for the cause, for the Scarlet Guard. Corporal Eastree and Barrow would be invaluable to us, not to mention they're both risking their lives to get me the information I need. The Guard owes them an oath, if not evacuation in Stage 2.

They're aren't here, in the thick of things, I tell myself. It helps ease the sting of disobedience. The Colonel and Command don't understand what Corvium means to the Nortan military, or how important our information will become. The tunnel system alone is worth my time—it connects every piece of the fortress city, allowing not only clandestine troop movements but easy infiltration of Corvium itself. And thanks to Barrow's position as aide to a high-ranking Silver, we know less-savory intelligence as well. Which officers prefer the unwilling company of Red soldiers. That Lord General Osanos, the nymph governor of the Westlakes region and commander of the city, continues a family feud with Lord General Laris, commander of the entire Nortan Air Fleet. Who is essential to the military and who wears rank for show. The list goes on. Petty rivalries and weaknesses to be exploited. There are places of rot for us to poke at.

If Command doesn't see this, then they must be blind.

But I am not.

And today is the day I set foot inside the walls myself and see the worst of what Norta has to offer tomorrow's revolution.

Cara folds up her broadcaster and reattaches it to the cord around her neck. It stays with her always, nestled next to her heart. "Not even to the Colonel?" she asks. "To gloat?"

"Not today." I force my best smirk. It placates her.

And it convinces me. The last two weeks have been a goldmine of information. The next two will certainly be the same.

I force my way out of the stuffy, shuttered closet we use for transmissions, the only part of the abandoned house with four walls and an intact roof. The rest of the structure does its job well, serving as the safe house for our dealings in Corvium. The main room, as long as it is wide, has brick walls, though one side is collapsed along with the rusted tin roof. And the smaller chamber, probably a bedroom, has no roof at all. Not that we mind. The Scarlet Guard has suffered worse, and the nights have been unseasonably warm, albeit humid. Summer is coming to Norta. Our plastic tents keep out the rain, but not the moist air. *It's nothing,* I tell myself. *A mild discomfort.* But sweat drips down my neck anyway. *And it's not even midday yet.*

Trying to ignore the sticky sensation that comes with the rising humidity, I pile my braid on top of my head, wrapping it like a crown. If this weather keeps up, I might just cut it all off.

"He's late," Tristan says from his lookout at a glassless window. His eyes never still, always darting, searching.

"I'd be worried if he wasn't." Barrow hasn't been on time once in the past two weeks, not for any of our meetings.

Cara joins Tye in the corner, dropping down with a merry flop. She sets to cleaning her glasses as intently as Tye cleans pistols. Both of them share the same look, fair-haired Lakelanders. Like me, they're not used to the May heat, and they cluster together in the shade.

Tristan is not so affected. He's a Piedmont boy originally, a son of mild winter and swampy summer. The heat doesn't bother him. In fact the only indicator of the changing season are his freckles, which seem to breed. They dot his arms and face, more every day. And his hair is longer too, a dark red mop that curls in the humidity.

"I told him as much," Rasha says from the opposite corner. She busies herself braiding her hair out of her dark face, taking care to divide her curling black locks into even pieces. Her own rifle, not so long as Tristan's but just as well used, props against the wall next to her. "Starting to think they don't sleep down in Piedmont."

"If you want to know more about my sleeping habits, all you have to do is ask, Rasha," Tristan replies. This time he turns over his shoulder, just for a second, to meet her black eyes. They share a knowing look.

I fight the urge to scoff. "Keep it to the woods, you two," I mutter. *Hard enough sleeping on the ground without listening to rustling tents.* "Scouts still out?"

"Tarry and Shore are taking the ridge, they won't be back until dusk, same as Big Coop and Martenson." Tristan ticks off the rest of our team on his fingers. "Cristobel and Little Coop are about a mile out, in the trees. Waiting on your Barrow boy, and looking to wait awhile."

I nod. All in order then.

"Command happy so far?"

"Happy as they can be," I lie as smoothly as I can. Thankfully, Tristan doesn't turn from his watch. He doesn't notice the flush I feel creeping up my neck. "We're feeding good intelligence. Worth our time for sure."

"They looking to oath Eastree or Barrow?"

"What makes you say that?"

He shrugs. "Seems like a long time to put into a pair we don't mean to recruit. Or are you suggesting them for Stage Two?"

Tristan doesn't mean to pry. He's a good lieutenant, the best I've ever seen, loyal to his bones. He doesn't know what he's picking at, but it stings all the same.

"Still working that out," I mumble, doing my best to walk slow as I run from his questions. "I'm going to do a turn around the property. Grab me if Barrow shows his face."

"Will do, boss," echoes from the room.

Keeping my steps even is a battle, and it seems like an eternity before I'm safely into the green trees. I heave a single collecting breath, forcing myself to calm down. *It's for the best. Lying to them, disobeying the orders, it's for the best. It's not your fault the Colonel doesn't understand. It's not your fault.* The old refrain levels me out, as comforting as a stiff drink. Everything I've done and everything I will do is for the cause. No one can say otherwise. No one will ever question my loyalty, not once I give them Norta on a silver platter.

A smile slowly replaces my usual scowl. My team doesn't know what's coming. Not even Tristan. They don't know what Command has planned for this kingdom in the coming weeks, or what we've done to put things in motion. Grinning, I remember the whirring video camera. The words I said in front of it. Soon, the world will hear them.

I don't like the woods here. They're too still, too quiet, with the smell of ash still clinging to the air. Despite the living trees, this is a dead place.

"Nice time for a walk."

My pistol jams against his temple before I have time to think.

Somehow, Barrow doesn't flinch. He only raises his palms in mock surrender.

"You're a special kind of stupid," I say.

He chuckles. "Must be, since I keep wandering back to your ragtag rebel club."

"*And* you're late."

"I prefer *chronologically challenged.*"

With a humorless scoff, I holster the gun, but keep my hand on it. I narrow my eyes at him. Usually his uniform is turned inside out for camouflage, but this time he hasn't bothered. His jacket is red as blood, dark and worn. He sticks out against the greenery.

"I've got two spotters waiting on you."

"They must not be very good." Again, that smile. Another would think Shade Barrow was warm, open, always laughing. But there's a chill beneath all that. An iron cold. "I came the usual way."

Sneering, I pat his jacket. "Did you now?"

There. His eyes flash, chips of frozen amber. Shade Barrow has secrets of his own. Just like everyone else.

"Let me tell my crew you're here," I press on, taking a step back from Barrow's lean form. His eyes follow my movements, quietly assessing. He's only nineteen, little more than a year into his military service, but his training certainly stuck.

"You mean tell your watchdog."

A corner of my mouth lifts. "His name is Tristan."

"Tristan, right. Ginger hair, permanently glued to his rifle." Barrow gives me my space, but follows all the same as I pick back toward the farmhouse. "Funny, I never expected to find a Southie embedded with you."

"Southie?" My voice doesn't quaver, despite Barrow's not-so-vague probing.

His pace quickens, until he's almost stepping on my heels. I fight the urge to kick back into his knee. "He's from Piedmont. Has to be, with his drawl. Not that it's much of a secret. Just like the rest of your bunch. All Lakelanders, yeah?"

I glance over my shoulder. "What gave you that idea?"

"And you're from the deep north, I suppose. Farther than our maps go," he presses on. I get the feeling he enjoys this, like a puzzle. "You're in for some fun come true summer, when the days run long and thick with heat. Nothing like a week of storm clouds that never break, and air that threatens to drown."

"No wonder you're not a trench soldier," I say as we reach the door. "There's no need for a poet on the front lines."

The bastard actually *winks* at me. "Well, we can't all be brutes."

In spite of Tristan's many warnings, I follow Barrow unarmed. If I'm caught in Corvium, I can plead as a simple Red Nortan in the wrong place at the wrong time. But not if I'm carrying my Lakelander pistol or a well-worn hunting knife. Then it'll be execution on the spot, not only for bearing arms without permission, but for being a Lakelander to boot. They'd probably slap me in front of a whisper for good measure, and that is the worst fate of all.

While most cities sprawl, with smaller towns and neighborhoods ringing round their walls and boundaries, Corvium stands alone. Barrow stops just before the end of the tree line, looking north at the cleared landscape around a hill. My eyes scan over the fortress city, noting anything of use. I've pored over the stolen maps of Corvium, but seeing it with my own eyes is something else entirely.

Black granite walls, spiked with gleaming iron, as well as other "weapons" to be harnessed by Silver abilities. Green vines thick as columns coil up the dozen or so watchtowers, a moat of dark water fed by piping rings the entire city, and strange mirrors dot between the metal prongs fanging the parapets. For Silver shadows, I assume, to concentrate their ability to harness light. And of course, there are more traditional weapons to take stock of. The oil-dark watchtowers bristle with grounded heavy guns, artillery ready to fire on any- and everything in the vicinity. And behind the walls, the buildings rise high, made tall by the cramped space. They too are black, tipped in gold and silver, a shadow beneath brightest sunlight. According to the maps, the city itself is organized like a wheel, with roads like spokes, all branching from the central square used to muster armies and stage executions.

The Iron Road marches straight through the city, from east to west. The western Road is quiet. No marching this late in the afternoon. But the eastern Road bustles with transports, most of them Silver-issue, carrying blue-blushing nobles and officers away from the fortress. The last, the slowest, is a Red delivery convoy returning to the markets of Rocasta, the nearest supply city. It consists of servants in wheeled transports, in horse-drawn carts, even on foot, all making the twenty-five-mile journey only to return again in a few days. I fish the spyglass from my jacket and hold it to my eye, following the ragged train.

A dozen transports, as many carts, maybe thirty Reds walking. All slow, keeping pace with each other. It'll take them at least nine hours to get where they're going. A waste of manpower, but I doubt they mind. Delivering uniforms is safer than wearing them. As I watch, the last of the convoy leaves the eastern gate.

"The Prayer Gate," Barrow mutters.

"Hmm?"

He taps my glass, then points. "We call it the Prayer Gate. As you enter, you pray to leave. As you leave, you pray never to return."

I can't help but scoff. "I didn't know Norta found religion." He only shakes his head. "Then who do you pray to?"

"No one, I guess. Just words, at the end of it all."

Somehow, in the shadow of Corvium, Shade Barrow's eyes find a bit of warmth.

"You get me in that gate, I'll teach you a prayer of my own." *Rise, Red as the Dawn.* Annoying as Barrow might be, I have a sneaking feeling he'll be Scarlet soon enough.

He tips his head, watching me as keenly as I watch him. "Deal."

"Although I don't see how you plan to do it. Our best chance was that convoy, but unfortunately you're—what did you say? Chronologically challenged?"

"No one's perfect, not even me," he replies with a shit-eating grin. "But I said I'd get you inside today, and I mean what I say. Eventually."

I look him up and down, gauging his manner. I do not trust Barrow. It's not in me to truly trust anyone. *But risk is part of the game.* "Are you going to get me shot?"

His grin widens. "I guess you'll have to find out."

"Well then, how do we do this?"

To my surprise, he extends a long-fingered hand. I stare at it, confused. *Does he mean to skip up to the gates like a pair of giggling children?* Frowning, I cross my arms and turn my back.

"Well, let's get moving—"

A curtain of black blots my vision as Barrow slips a scarf over my eyes.

I would scream if I could, signaling to Tristan following us from a quarter mile away. But the air is suddenly crushed from my lungs and everything seems to shrink. I feel nothing but the tightening world and the warm bulk of Barrow's chest against my back. Time spins, everything falls. The ground tips beneath my feet.

I hit concrete hard, enough to rattle an already rattling brain. The blindfold slips off, not that it does me much good. My vision spots, black against something darker, all of it still spinning. I have to shut my eyes again to convince myself I'm not spinning with it.

My hands scrabble against something slick and cold—hopefully water—as I try to push myself back up. Instead, I fall backward, and force my eyes open to find blue, dank darkness. The spots recede, slow at first, then all at once.

"What the f—!"

I turn onto my knees, throwing up everything in my belly.

Barrow's hand finds my back, rubbing what he assumes are soothing circles. But his touch makes my skin crawl. I spit, finished retching, and force myself to uneasy feet, if only to get away from him.

He puts out a hand to steady me but I smack it away, wishing I'd kept my knife.

"Don't touch me," I snarl. "What was that? What happened? *Where am I?*"

"Careful, you're turning into a philosopher."

I spit acidic bile at his feet. "Barrow!" I hiss.

He sighs, annoyed as a schoolteacher. "I took you through the pipe tunnels. There's a few in the tree line. Had to keep you blinded, of course. Can't let all my secrets go for free."

"Pipes my ass. We were standing outside a minute ago. Nothing moves that fast."

Barrow tries his best to smother a grin. "You hit your head," he says after a long moment. "Passed out on the slide down."

That would explain the vomiting. *Concussion.* Yet I've never felt so alert. All the pain and nausea of the last few seconds are suddenly gone.

Gingerly, I feel along my skull, searching for a bump or a tender spot. But there's nothing at all.

He watches my examination with strangely focused attention. "Or do you think you ended up a half mile away, beneath the fortress of Corvium, some other way?"

"No, I suppose not."

As my eyes adjust to the gloom, I realize we're in a supply cellar. Abandoned or forgotten, judging by the dust on the empty shelves and the inch of standing water on the floor. I avoid looking at the fresh pile of sick.

"Here, put these on." He fishes a grimy bundle of cloth from somewhere in the dark, carefully hidden but easy to find. It sails my way, colliding with my chest in a puff of dust and odor.

"Wonderful," I mutter, unfolding it to find a regulation uniform. It's well worn, patched and stained with who-knows-what. The insignia is simple, a single white bar outlined in black. An infantry soldier, enlisted. *A walking corpse.* "Whose body did you swipe this off?"

The shock of cold sparks in him again, only for a moment. "It'll fit. That's all you need to worry about."

"Very well."

I shrug out of my jacket without much fanfare, then peel off my battered pants and shirt in succession. My undergarments are nothing special, mismatched and thankfully clean, but Barrow stares anyway, his mouth open a little.

"Catching flies, Barrow?" I taunt as I pull on the uniform trousers. In the dim light, they look red and battered as rusted pipes.

"Sorry," he mutters, turning his head, then his body. As if I care about privacy. I smirk at the blush spreading up his neck.

"I didn't think soldiers were so embarrassed by the female form," I press on as I zip myself into the uniform top. It's snug but fits well enough. Obviously meant for someone shorter, with narrower shoulders.

He whips back around. The flush has reached his cheeks. It makes him seem younger. *No,* I realize. *It makes him seem his age.* "I didn't know Lakelanders were so free with them."

I flash him a smile as cold as his eyes. "I'm Scarlet Guard, boy. We have worse things to worry about than naked flesh."

Something trembles between us. A current of air maybe, or perhaps the ache of my head injury finally coming back. *That must be it.*

Then Barrow laughs.

"What?"

"You remind me of my sister."

It's my turn to grin. "You spy on her a lot, do you?"

He doesn't flinch at the jab, letting it glance past. "In your manner, Farley. Your ways. You think the same."

"She must be a bright girl."

"She certainly thinks so."

"Very funny."

"I think you two would be great friends." Then he tips his head, pausing a second. "Or you might kill each other."

For the second time in as many minutes, I reluctantly touch Barrow. This is not so gentle as his hands on my back. Instead, I punch him lightly on the arm. "Let's get moving," I tell him. "I don't fancy standing around in a dead woman's clothes."

THE FOLLOWING MESSAGE HAS BEEN DECODED
CONFIDENTIAL, SENIOR CLEARANCE REQUIRED

—Captain, return to orders. COMMAND won't stand for this. —RAM—

THE FOLLOWING MESSAGE HAS BEEN DECODED
CONFIDENTIAL, COMMAND CLEARANCE REQUIRED

Day 29 of Operation SHIELDWALL, Stage 2.
Operative: Colonel REDACTED.
Designation: RAM.
Origin: REDACTED.
Destination: DRUMMER at REDACTED.

-No contact from LAMB in 2 days.
-Request permission to intercept.
-SHIELDWALL ahead of schedule. Island #3 operational but transit
problematic. More boats needed than previously thought.

RISE, RED AS THE DAWN.

THE FOLLOWING MESSAGE HAS BEEN DECODED
CONFIDENTIAL, SENIOR CLEARANCE REQUIRED

Operative: General REDACTED.
Designation: DRUMMER.
Origin: COMMAND at REDACTED.
Destination: RAM at REDACTED.

-Permission to intercept granted, will relay further info re. her location.
-Use force if necessary. She was your suggestion and your mistake if
things continue.
-Get RED WEB to Stage 2. Collab with other teams to begin removal.
-Will explore other transit options for #3.

RISE, RED AS THE DAWN.

THE FOLLOWING MESSAGE HAS BEEN DECODED
CONFIDENTIAL, SENIOR CLEARANCE REQUIRED

—LAMB get your ass in line, or it's your head. —RAM—

Another message to the fire.

"Charming," I mutter, watching the Colonel's words burn up.

This time, Cara doesn't bother to ask. But her lips purse into a thin line, holding back a torrent of questions. Five days now since I've responded to any messages, official or otherwise. She obviously knows something is afoot.

"Cara—," I begin, but she holds up a hand.

"I don't have clearance," she replies. Her eyes meet mine with startling ferocity. "And I don't care to know what path you're leading us down, so long as you think it's the right one."

A warmth fills my insides. I do my best to keep it from showing, but a bit of a smile bleeds out anyways. My hand finds her shoulder, offering her the smallest touch of thanks.

"Don't get sappy on me now, Captain." She chuckles, tucking away the broadcaster.

"Will do." I straighten, turning around to face the rest of my team. They cluster at the edge of the steaming alley, a respectful distance away to allow for my private correspondences. To hide our presence, Tristan and Rasha sit on the alley curb, facing the street beyond. They keep their hands out and their hoods up, begging for food or money. Everyone slides past, looking elsewhere.

"Tye, Big Coop." The pair in question steps forward. Tye tips her head, pointing her good ear at me, while Big Coop lives up to the nick-name. With a chest like a barrel and almost seven feet of heavy muscle, he's nearly twice the size of his brother, Little Coop. "Stay with Cara, keep the second radio ready."

She extends a hand, all but itching to get hold of our newest prize. One of three top-of-the-line, techie-made, long-range secure radios, all swiped from the Corvium stores by Barrow's light fingers. I pass along the radio, though I keep the second tucked close. Barrow kept the third. Should he need to get in touch. Not that he's used it yet. Not that I'm keeping tally of his communications. Usually Barrow just shows up when he wants to trade information, always without warning, slipping past every spotter I put around the farmhouse. But today we're beyond even his sly reach. Twenty-five miles east, in the middle of Rocasta.

"As for the rest. Cristobel, Little Coop, you're on over watch. Get high, get hidden. Usual signals."

Cris grins, showing a mouth of missing teeth. Punishment for "smirking" at her Silver master, back when she was a twelve-year-old serving girl in a Trial mansion. Little Coop is just as eager. His size and mousy demeanor, not to mention his brick wall of a brother, hide a skilled operative with a steel spine. Needing nothing more, they set to their work. Little Coop picks a drain pipe, scrabbling up the brick walls of the alley, while Cris scrambles to a fence, using it to boost herself onto a narrow window ledge. Both disappear in moments, to follow us from the Rocastan rooftops.

"The rest of you, track your marks. Keep your ears open. Memorize movements. I want to know everything from birthdays to shoe sizes. Gather whatever you can in the time we can." The words are familiar. Everyone knows why I called for this scout. But it serves as a rallying cry, one last thread drawing us together. *Tying them to your disobedience, you mean.*

My fist curls, nails digging into my palm where no one can see. The sting erases the thought quite nicely. As does the breeze sweeping through the alley. It stinks of garbage, but it's cool at least, blowing off Lake Eris to the north.

"The more we know about the Corvium supply convoy, the easier it'll be to infiltrate." *As good a reason as any to be here, to stay when all the Colonel does is tell me to leave.* "Gates close at sundown. Return to rally point within the hour. Understood?"

Their heads bob in taut unison, their eyes alive, bright, and eager.

A few blocks away, a clock tower chimes nine times. I move without thought, stepping through my Guardsmen as they fall in line behind me. Tristan and Rasha are the last to stand. My lieutenant looks bare without his rifle, but I know there's a pistol on him somewhere, probably collecting sweat at the base of his back.

We head into the street, a main avenue through the Red sector of the city. Safe for now, surrounded by nothing more than Red homes and businesses, with few if any Silver officers to watch us pass. As in Harbor Bay, Rocasta maintains its own Red Watch, to protect what Silvers won't. Though we're heading for the same place, my team splits into their pairs, putting space between us. Can't exactly rove into the city center looking like a jumped-up assault squad, let alone a gang. Tristan keeps close again, letting me lead us to our destination—the Iron Road. As in Corvium, the Road bisects Rocasta, driving right through its heart like river through valley. As we get closer to the main thoroughfare, traffic picks up. Late servants hurrying to the homes of their masters, volunteer watchmen returning from their night posts, parents hustling their children to ramshackle schools.

And of course, more officers with every passing street. Their uniforms, black with silver trim, are severe in the harsh sun of late spring, as are the gleaming guns and clubs at their waists. Funny, they feel the need to wear uniforms, as if they're at risk of being mistaken for Red. One of us. *Not a chance.* Their skin, undershot with blue and gray, leached of everything alive, is distinguishing enough. There is no Red on earth so cold as a Silver.

Ten yards ahead of us, Rasha stops so quickly her partner, Martenson, almost trips over her. No mean feat, considering she has about six inches on the graying Little Papa. Next to me, Tristan tenses, but doesn't break formation. He knows the rules. Nothing is above the Guard, not even affection.

The Silver legionnaires drag a boy by the arms. His feet kick at open air. He's small, looking young for eighteen. I doubt he needs to shave. I do my best to block out the sound of his begging, but his mother's wail cannot be ignored. She follows, two more children on her heels, with a solemn father trailing behind. Her hands clutch at her son's shirt, offering one last bout of resistance to his conscription.

The street seems to hold its breath as one, watching the familiar tragedy.

A crack echoes and she falls backward, clutching a bruising cheek. The legionnaire didn't even lift a finger or even look up from his grim work. He must be a telkie and used his abilities to swat the woman away.

"You want worse?" he snaps when she moves to stand.

"Don't!" the boy says, using his last free words to beg.

This will not last. This will not continue. This is why I'm here.

Even so, it makes me sick to know I cannot do anything for this boy and his mother. Our plans are falling into place, but not fast enough for him. *Perhaps he will survive*, I tell myself. But one look at his thin arms and the eyeglasses trampled beneath a legionnaire's foot says otherwise. The boy will die like so many others. In a trench or in a wasteland, alone at the very end.

"I can't watch this," I mutter, and turn down another alley.

After a long moment of strange hesitation, Tristan follows.

I can only hope Rasha stays the course as well as he does. But I understand. She lost two sisters to Lakelander conscriptions, and fled her home before meeting the same fate.

Rocasta is not a walled city, and has no gates to choke the ends of the Iron Road. An easy place to enter, but it makes our task a bit more difficult. The main body of the returning supply convoy comes along the Road, but a few of the walking escorts peel off, taking different shortcuts to the same destination. On another day, my team would spend hours tracking them all to their homes, only to watch them sleep off the long journey. Not so now. Because it's First Friday. Today is the Feat of July.

A ridiculous Nortan tradition, albeit an effective one, if the intelligence is to be believed. Arenas in almost every town and city, casting long shadows and spitting blood once a month. Reds are required to attend, to sit and watch Silver champions exchange blows and abilities with the glee of stage performers. We have no such thing in the Lakelands. Silvers don't feel the need to show off against us, and the storied threat of Norta is enough to keep everyone terrified.

"They do it in Piedmont too," Tristan mutters. He leans against the poured concrete fence edging the promenade around the arena's entrance. Our gazes flick in unison, one of us always watching our marks, another always watching the band of officers directing people into the gaping maw of Arena Rocasta.

"Call them Acts, not Feats. And we didn't just have to watch. Sometimes, they made Reds fight too." I hear the tremor of rage in his voice, even above the organized chaos of today's spectacle.

I nudge his shoulder as gently as I can. "Fight each other?" *Kill Reds, or be killed by Silvers?* I don't know which is worse.

"Targets are moving," he simply growls.

One more glance at the officers, now occupied with a band of mangy kids halting foot traffic. "Let's go." *And let that wound fester with the rest.*

I push off the wall next to him and slip into the crowd, eyes trained on the four red uniforms up ahead. It isn't easy. This close to Corvium, there's a lot of Red military, either marching through to take their places in the Choke or attached to different convoys like the one we're tailing. But the four men, three bronze, one dark skinned, all bone tired, keep close to each other. We haunt their footsteps. They manned a horse cart for the convoy, carrying what, I'm not sure. It was empty when they returned with the rest. But judging by the lack of Security and Silvers, I know their supply train isn't for weaponry or ammunition. The three bronze men are brothers, I assume, judging by their similar faces and mannerisms. It's almost comical to watch them spit and scratch their behinds in staggered unison. The fourth, a burly fellow with vividly blue eyes, is subdued in his itching, though he smiles more than the rest put together. Crance, I think his name is, based on my eavesdropping.

We enter the arches of the arena entrance like prowling cats, close enough to hear our marks but not be noticed. Overhead, harsh electric lights flicker, illuminating the high-ceilinged chamber connecting the outer promenade to the interior. The crowd thickens to our left, where a variety of Reds wait to place their bets on the ensuing match. Above it, the boards announce the Silvers to fight, and their odds of victory.

Flora Lerolan, Oblivion, 3/1

Maddux Thany, Stoneskin, 10/1

"Hang on a second," Crance says, halting the rest by the betting boards. With a grin, one of the bronze men joins him. The pair dig in their pockets for something to gamble.

Under the pretense of doing the same, Tristan and I stop no more than a few feet away, hidden in the swelling crowd. The betting boards are popular among the Reds of Rocasta, where a thriving military economy keeps most from going hungry. There are several well-to-do among the crowd—merchants and business owners in proudly clean clothes. They make their bets and hand over dull coppers, even a few silver tetrarchs. I bet the till of Arena Rocasta is nothing to sneer at, and make a note to pass on such information to Command. *If they'll still listen to me.*

"Come on, look at the odds—it's easy money!" Still smiling infectiously, Crance points between the boards and the betting windows. The other two tailing along don't look so convinced.

"You know something about stoneskins we don't?" the tallest says. "He'll get blown to pebbles by the oblivion."

"Suit yourself, Horner. But I didn't trudge all the way from Corvium to sit bored in the stands." Bills in hand, Crance slips away with his friend on his heels, leaving Horner and the other man to wait. Somehow, despite Crance's size, he's surprisingly good at cutting through a crowd. Too good.

"Watch them," I murmur with a touch to Tristan's elbow. And then I'm weaving too, careful to keep my head angled at the ground. There are cameras here, enough to be wary of. Should the next few weeks go as planned, I might want to start hiding my face.

I see it as Crance passes his paper through the window. His sleeve lifts as it scrapes the betting ledge, pulling back to reveal a tattoo. It almost blends into his umber skin, but the shape is unmistakable. I've seen it before. Blue anchor. Red rope.

We're not the only crew working this convoy. The Mariners already have a man inside.

This is good. We can work with this. My mind fires as I fight my way back. *Pay for their information. Less Guard involvement, but the same outcome. And odds are the Mariner is alone, working the job solo. We could try to turn him, get our own eyes inside the Mariners. Start pulling strings, absorb the gang into the Guard.*

Tristan stands a head above the crowd, still watching the other two marks. I fight the urge to sprint to his side and divulge everything.

But an obstacle sprouts between us. A bald man and a familiar sheen of sweat across his brow. *Lakelander.* Before I can run or shout, a hand closes around my throat from behind. Tight enough to keep me quiet, loose enough to let me breathe, and certainly enough to drag me through the crowd with Baldy keeping close.

Another might thrash or fight, but I know better. Silver officers are everywhere here, and their "help" is not anything I want to risk. Instead I put my trust in myself, and in Tristan. He must keep watch, and I must get free.

The crowd takes us in its current, and still I cannot see who it is marching me through. Baldy's bulk hides most of me, as does the scarf my captor tosses around my neck. Funny, it's scarlet. And then we climb. Up the steps, high above the arena floor, to long slab seats that are mostly abandoned.

Only then am I released, pushed to sit.

I whirl in a fury, fists clenched and ready, only to find the Colonel staring back, very much prepared for my rage.

"You want to add striking your commanding officer to your list of offenses?" he says. It's almost a purr.

No, I don't. Glumly, I drop my fists. Even if I could fight my way past Baldy, I don't want to try myself at the Colonel and his wiry strength. I raise a hand to my neck instead, massaging the now tender skin beneath the red scarf.

"It won't bruise," he continues.

"Your mistake. I thought you wanted to send a message. Nothing says 'get your ass back in line' like a blue neck."

His red eye flashes. "You stop responding and think I'll let that go? Not a chance, Captain. Now tell me what's going on here. What of your team? Have you all gone rogue, or did some run off?"

"No one's run off," I force through gritted teeth. "Not one of them. No one's rogue either. They're still following orders."

"At least someone is."

"I am still under operation, whether you choose to see it or not. Everything I'm doing here is for the cause, for the Guard. Like you said, this isn't the Lakelands. And while getting the Whistle network online is priority, so is Corvium." I have to hiss to be heard over the crowding arena. "We can't rely on the slow creep here. Things are too centralized. People will notice, and they'll root us out before we're ready. We have to hit hard, hit big, hit where the Silvers can't hide us."

I'm gaining ground, but not much. Still, it's enough for him to keep his voice from shaking. He's angry, but not livid. He can still be reasoned with.

"That's precisely what you recorded for," he says. "You remember, I assume."

A camera and a red scarf across half my face. A gun in one hand, a newly made flag in the other, reciting words memorized like a prayer. *And we will rise up, Red as the dawn.*

"Farley, this is how we operate. No one holds all the cards. No one knows the hand. It's the only way we stay ahead and alive," he presses on. From another, it might sound like pleading. But not the Colonel. He doesn't ask things. He just orders. "But believe me when I say, we have plans for Norta. And they aren't so far from what you want."

Below us, the champions of the Feat march out onto the strange gray sand. One, the Thany stoneskin, has a boulder belly, and is nearly as wide as he is tall. He has no need for armor, and is naked to the waist. For her part, the oblivion looks every inch her ability. Dressed in interlocking plates of red and orange, she dances like a nimble flame.

"And do those plans include Corvium?" I whisper, turning back to the Colonel. I must make him understand. "Do you think me so blind that I wouldn't notice if there was another operation in this city? Because there isn't. There's no one here but me. No one else seems to care about that fortress where every single Red doomed to die passes through. *Every single one.* And you think that place isn't important?"

Corporal Eastree flashes in my head. Her gray face and gray eyes, her stern resolve. She spoke of slavery, because that's what this world is. No one dares say it, but that's what Reds are. *Slaves and graves.*

For once, the Colonel holds his tongue. *Good, or else I might cut it out.*

"You go back to Command and you tell someone else to continue with Red Web. Oh, and let them know the Mariners are here too. They're not so shortsighted as the rest of us."

Part of me expects to be slapped for insubordination. In all our years, I've never spoken to him like this. Not even—not even in the north. At the frozen place we all used to call home. But I was a child then. A little girl pretending to be a hunter, gutting rabbits and setting bad snares to feel important. I am not her anymore. I am twenty-two years old, a captain of the Scarlet Guard, and no one, not even the Colonel, can tell me I am wrong now.

"Well?"

After a long, trembling moment, he opens his mouth. "No."

An explosion below matches my rage. The crowd gasps in time with the fight, watching as the wispy oblivion tries to live up to her odds. But the Mariner was right. The stoneskin will win. He is a mountain against her fire, and he will endure.

"My team will stand with me," I warn. "You'll lose ten good soldiers and one captain to your pride, Colonel."

"No, Captain, someone else is not going to take over Red Web from you," he says. "But I will petition Command for a Corvium operation, and when they've secured a team, it will take your place."

When. Not if. I can barely believe what he's saying.

"Until such time, you will remain in Corvium and continue work with your contacts. Relay all pertinent information through the usual channels."

"But Command—"

"Command is more open-minded than you know. And for whatever reason, they think the world of you."

"I can't tell if you're lying."

He merely raises one shoulder, shrugging. His eyes rove back to the arena floor, to watch as the stoneskin rips the young oblivion apart.

Somehow, his reason grates on me more than anything else. It's hard to hate him in a time like this, when I remember who he used to be. And then of course, I remember the rest. What he did to us, to our family. To my mother and sister, who were not so horrible as we were, who could not survive in the monster he made.

I wish he wasn't my father. I've wished it so many times.

"How goes Shieldwall?" I murmur to keep my thoughts at bay.

"Ahead of schedule." Not a hint of pride, just sober fact. "But transit could be an issue, once we set in on removal."

Supposedly the second stage of my operation. The removal and transport of *assets* deemed useful to the Scarlet Guard. Not just Reds who would pledge to the cause but ones who can fire a gun, drive a transport, read, fight.

"I shouldn't know—," I begin, but he cuts me off. I get the feeling he doesn't have anyone to talk to, if Baldy is any indication. *Now that I'm gone.*

"Command gave me three boats. *Three.* They think three boats can help get an entire island populated and working."

Somewhere in my brain, a bell rings. And on the floor, the stoneskin raises his rocky arms, victorious. Skin healers tend to the oblivion girl, fixing up her broken jaw and crushed shoulders with quick touches. *Crance will be happy.*

"Does Command ever mention pilots?" I wonder aloud.

The Colonel turns, one eyebrow raised. "Pilots? For what?"

"I think my man inside Corvium can get us something better than boats, or at least, a way to steal something better than boats."

Another man would smile, but the Colonel simply nods.

"Do it."

THE FOLLOWING MESSAGE HAS BEEN DECODED
CONFIDENTIAL, COMMAND CLEARANCE REQUIRED

Operative: Colonel REDACTED.

Designation: RAM.

Origin: Rocasta, NRT.

Destination: COMMAND at REDACTED

-Contact made with LAMB. Her team still online, no losses.

-Assessment: CORVIUM worth an operation team. Suggest MERCY.
Suggest a rush. LAMB will hand off and return to RED WEB.

-LAMB passing intelligence vital to SHIELDWALL and removal/transit.

-Returning to post.

RISE, RED AS THE DAWN.

THE FOLLOWING MESSAGE HAS BEEN DECODED
CONFIDENTIAL, SENIOR CLEARANCE REQUIRED

Operative: General REDACTED.

Designation: DRUMMER.

Origin: COMMAND at REDACTED.

Destination: RAM at REDACTED, LAMB at Corvium, NRT.

-CORVIUM suggestion under advisement.

-Captain Farley will return to RED WEB in two days.

-COMMAND split on punishment as is.

-Awaiting intelligence.

RISE, RED AS THE DAWN.

THE FOLLOWING MESSAGE HAS BEEN DECODED

CONFIDENTIAL, SENIOR CLEARANCE REQUIRED

Operative: Captain REDACTED.
Designation: LAMB.
Origin: Corvium, NRT.
Destination: RAM at REDACTED, COMMAND at REDACTED.

-Request a week.

RISE, RED AS THE DAWN.

—You're a special kind of stupid, kid. —RAM—

THE FOLLOWING MESSAGE HAS BEEN DECODED
CONFIDENTIAL, SENIOR CLEARANCE REQUIRED

Operative: General REDACTED.
Designation: DRUMMER.
Origin: COMMAND at REDACTED.
Destination: RAM at REDACTED, LAMB at Corvium, NRT.

-Five days. No more negotiation.

RISE, RED AS THE DAWN.

Somehow the farmhouse has begun to feel like a home.

Even with the collapsed roof, the tents wicked with humidity, and the silence of the woods. It's the longest I've been anywhere since

Irabelle, but that was always base. And while the soldiers there are the closest thing I have to family, I never could see the cold concrete and mazelike passages as anything more than a way station. A place to train and wait for the next assignment.

Not so with the ruin on the doorstep of the killing grounds, in the shadow of a grave city.

"That's it," I tell Cara, and lean back against the closet wall.

She nods and folds away the broadcaster. "Nice to see you all chatting again."

Before I can laugh, Tristan's neat knock jars the shuttered excuse for a door. "Got company."

Barrow.

"Duty calls," I grumble as I scoot past Cara, bumping her in the closed space. Wrenching open the door, I'm surprised to find Tristan standing so close, his usual nervous energy on overdrive.

"Spotters got him this time, finally," he says. On another day, he might be proud, but something about this sets him off. I know why. We never see Barrow coming. *So why today?* "Signaled it's important—"

Behind him, the farmhouse door bangs open, revealing a red-faced Barrow flanked by Cris and Little Coop.

One look at his terrified face is enough.

"Scatter," I snap.

They know what it means. They know where to go.

A hurricane moves through the farmhouse, taking home with it. The guns, the provisions, our gear disappears in a practiced heartbeat, shoved into bags and packs. Cris and Little Coop are already gone, into the trees, to get as high as they can. Their mirrors and birdcalls will carry the message to the others in the woods. Tristan supervises the rest, all while loading his long rifle.

"There isn't *time*, they're coming now!" Barrow hisses, suddenly at my side. He takes my elbow and not gently. "You have to go!"

Two snaps of my fingers. The team obeys, dropping whatever isn't packed away. I guess we'll have to steal some more tents down the line, but it's the least of my worries. Another snap, and they fly like bullets from a gun. Cara, Tye, Rasha, and the rest going through the door and the collapsed wall, in all directions with all speed. The woods swallow them whole.

Tristan waits for me because it's his job. Barrow waits because—because I don't know.

"*Farley*," he hisses. Another tug at my arm.

I cast one last glance, making sure we have everything, before making my own escape into the tree line. The men follow, keeping pace with my sprint through tangled roots and brush. My heart pounds in my ears, beating a harried drum. *We've had worse. We've had worse.*

Then I hear the dogs.

Animos-controlled hounds. They'll smell us, they'll follow, and the swifts will run us down. If we're lucky they'll think we're deserters and kill us in the forest. If not—I don't want to think about what horrors the black city of Corvium holds.

"Get to water," I force out. "They'll lose the scent!"

But the river is a half mile on.

I only hope they take the time to search the farmhouse, giving us the window we need to escape. At least the others are farther on, spread wide. No pack can follow us all. But me, us, the freshest, closest scent? Easy prey.

Despite the protest in my muscles, I push harder and run faster than

I ever have before. But after only a minute, *only a minute*, I start to tire. If only I could run as fast as my thundering heart.

Tristan slows with me, though he doesn't need to. "There's a creek," he hisses, pointing south. "Shoots off the river, closer. You head for it."

"What are you talking about?"

"I can make it to the river. You can't. And they can't follow us both."

My eyes widen. I almost trip in my confusion, but Barrow catches me before I can, sternly helping me over a gnarled root. "Tristan—"

My lieutenant only smiles and pats the gun slung across his back. Then he points. "That way, Boss."

Before I can stop him, before I can order him not to, he leaps through the trees, using his long legs and the lower branches to vault over worsening ground. I can't shout after him. Somehow I don't even get a good look at his face. Only a mop of red hair, gleaming through the green.

Barrow all but shoves me. I think he looks relieved, but that can't be right. Especially when a dog howls not a hundred yards away. And the trees above us seem to bow, their branches reaching like cloying fingers. *Greenwardens. Animosi. Swifts. The Silvers will catch us both.*

"Farley." Suddenly both his hands are on my jaw, forcing me to look at a shockingly calm face. There's fear, of course, flickering in his golden eyes. But not nearly enough for the situation. Not like me. I am terrified. "You have to promise not to scream."

"Wha—?"

"*Promise.*"

I see the first dog. A hound the size of a pony, its jowls dripping. And next to it, a gray blur like the wind made flesh. *Swift.*

Again, I feel the squeeze of Shade's body against mine, and then something less pleasant. The tightening of the world, the spin, the tipping forward through empty air. All of it compounds and contracts, and I think I see green stars. Or maybe trees. I feel a familiar wave of nausea first. This time I land in a streambed instead of on concrete.

I sputter, spitting water and bile, fighting the urge to scream or be sick or both.

Barrow crouches over me, one hand raised.

"Ah, don't scream."

Sick it is.

"I suppose that's preferable at the moment," he mutters, kindly looking anywhere but my green face. "Sorry, I guess I need more practice. Or maybe you're just sensitive."

The gurgling stream cleans up what I can't, and the cold water does more for me than a mug of black coffee. I snap to attention, looking around at the trees bowing over us. Willows, not oaks like where we were just seconds ago. *They're not moving*, I realized with a swell of relief. *No greenwardens here. No dogs either.* But then—*where are we?*

"How?" I whisper, my voice ragged. "Don't say pipes."

The practiced shield of Shade Barrow drops a little. He takes a few steps back from me so he can sit on a stone above the stream, perching like a gargoyle. "I don't quite have an explanation," he says as if he's admitting a crime. "The best—the best I can do is show you. And, again, you have to promise not to scream."

Dully, I nod. My head swims, still off balance. I can barely sit up in the stream, let alone shout.

He heaves a breath, his fingers gripping the stone until his knuckles turn white. "Okay."

And then he's gone. Not—not from running away or hiding or even falling off the rock. He just simply *isn't*. I blink, not believing what I see.

"Here."

My head turns so quickly I'm almost sick again.

There he is, standing on the opposite bank. Then he does it again, returning to the stone, taking a slow seat once more. He forces a tentative smile without any joy behind it. And his eyes are wide, so wide. If I was afraid a few minutes ago, he is completely petrified. And he should be.

Because Shade Barrow is Silver.

Muscle memory lets me draw my gun and cock the hammer without blinking.

"I might not be able to scream, but I can shoot you."

He flushes, somehow his face and neck turning red. *An illusion, a trick. His blood is not that color.*

"There's a few reasons why that won't work," he says, daring to look away from my pistol. "For one thing, your barrel's full of water. Two, in case you haven't noticed—"

Suddenly he's by my ear, crouching next to me in the stream. The shock of it raises a shriek, or at least it would if he didn't clamp a hand over my mouth. "—I'm pretty fast."

I'm dreaming. This isn't real.

He hauls my dazed body up, forcing me to stand. I try to shove him off but even that makes me dizzy.

"And three, the dogs might not be able to smell us anymore, but they can certainly hear a gunshot." His hands don't leave my shoulders, gripping each tightly. "So, are you going to rethink your little strategy, Captain?"

"You're Silver?" I breathe, turning in his grasp. This time I right myself before I fall. As in Corvium, the nausea is wearing off quickly. *A side effect of his ability. His Silver ability. He's done this to me before and*

I didn't even know it. The thought burns through my brain. "All this time?"

"No, no. I'm Red as that dawn thing you keep going on about."

"Don't lie to me." I still have the gun in hand. "This has all been a trick so you could catch us. I bet you led those hunters right to my team—!"

"I *said* no screaming." His mouth hangs open, drawing ragged breath past his teeth. He's so close I can see the blood vessels spindling through the whites of his eyes. They're red. *An illusion, a trick*, rings again. But memories of him come with the warning. How many times did he meet me alone? How many weeks has he worked with us, passing information, relaying with the blood-Red Corporal Eastree? How many times did he have the opportunity to spring a trap?

I can't. I can't make sense of this.

"And no one followed me. *Obviously* no one can follow me. They found out about you on their own. Something about spies in Rocasta, didn't quite catch it all."

"So you're still safe in Corvium, still *working* for them? As *one of them*?"

His patience snaps like a twig. "I told you, I'm not Silver!" he growls, an animal in that quaking second. I want to take a step backward, but force myself to stand firm, unmoving, unafraid of him. *Though I have every right to be.*

Then he shoves his arm out, drawing back the sleeve with shaking fingers. "Cut me." He nods, answering my question before I can ask. "Cut. Me."

To my surprise, my fingers shake just as badly as his when I draw the knife from my boot. He flinches when I press it to his skin. *At least he feels pain.*

My heart skips a beat when blood swells beneath the blade. *Red as the dawn.*

"How is this possible?"

I look up to find him staring at my face, looking for something. By the way his eyes flash, I think he finds it.

"I honestly don't know. I don't know what this is or what I am. I only know I'm not one of them. I'm one of *yours.*"

For a blistering moment, I forget my team, the woods, my mission, and even Shade standing in front of me. Again, the world tips, but not from anything he can do. This is something more. A shifting. A change. And a *weapon* to be used. *No, a weapon I've already wielded many times. To get information, to infiltrate Corvium. With Shade Barrow, the Scarlet Guard can go anywhere. Everywhere.*

You'd think, with all my breaches in protocol, I'd try to steer away from breaking any more rules. But at the same time, *what's one more going to do?*

Slowly, I close my fingers around his wrist. He still bleeds, but I don't mind. *It's fitting.*

"Will you oath yourself to the Scarlet Guard?"

I expect him to smile. Instead his face turns to stone.

"On one condition."

My eyebrows raise so high they might disappear into my hairline. "The Guard does not bargain."

"This isn't a request to the Guard, but to you," he replies. For a man who can move faster than the blink of an eye, somehow he manages to take the world's slowest step forward. We stand eye to eye, blue meeting gold.

Curiosity gets the better of me. "And that is?"

"What's your name?"

My name. The others don't mind using their own, but for me, there is no such thing. My name holds no importance. Only rank and designation truly matter. What my mother called me is of no consequence to anyone, least of all me. It is a burden more than anything, a stinging reminder of her voice and the life we lived in early days. When the Colonel was called Papa, and the Scarlet Guard was the pipe dream of hunters and farmers and empty soldiers. My name is my mother, my sister Madeline, and their graves dug in the frozen ground of a village no one lives in anymore.

Shade looks on, expectant. I realize he's holding my hand, not minding the blood coagulating beneath my fingers.

"My name is Diana."

For once, his smile is real. No jokes, no mask.

"Are you with us, Shade Barrow?"

"I'm with you, Diana."

"Then we will rise."

His voice joins mine.

"Red as the dawn."

THE FOLLOWING MESSAGE HAS BEEN DECODED
CONFIDENTIAL, SENIOR CLEARANCE REQUIRED

Day 34 of Operation RED WEB, Stage 1.
Operative: Captain REDACTED.
Designation: LAMB.
Origin: On the move.
Destination: RAM at REDACTED, COMMAND at REDACTED.

-Leaving CORVIUM, heading to DELPHIE. Stopping at WHISTLE points along route.

-Plan to be in Stage 2 within a week.

-Advise CORVIUM operation that CORVIUM officials believe there are "bandits and deserters" in the woods.

-Enclosed is detailed information about Air Fleet grounded in DELPHIE, procured by newly oathed operative Aide B (designation: SHADOW) still in CORVIUM.

-Suggest Corp E be oathed as well.

-I am and will remain SHADOW's SG contact.

-SHADOW will be removed from CORVIUM at my discretion.

-CORVIUM overview: Killed in action: G. TYE, W. TARRY, R. SHORE, C. ELSON, H. "Big" COOPER (5).
Missing in action: T. BOREEVE, R. BINLI (2).
Silver casualty count: Zero (0).

THE FOLLOWING MESSAGE HAS BEEN DECODED
CONFIDENTIAL, SENIOR CLEARANCE REQUIRED

Operative: General REDACTED.
Designation: DRUMMER.
Origin: COMMAND at REDACTED.
Destination: RAM at REDACTED.

-Air intel good. DELPHIE Operation in motion.

-Train transit online between ARCHEON and City #1.

-Begin 3 week countdown for Operation DAYBREAK.

RISE, RED AS THE DAWN.

—Your girl has balls. —DRUMMER—

—The girl gets our people killed. —RAM—

—Worth it for her results. But her attitude leaves something to be
desired. —DRUMMER—

Day 54 of Operation RED WEB, Stage 2.
Operative: Captain REDACTED.
Designation: LAMB.
Origin: Albanus, NRT.
Destination: RAM at REDACTED.

-CAPITAL VALLEY WHISTLES coming online. In ALBANUS to open
removal with oathed WHISTLE operative WILL.
-30 assets removed in 2 weeks.
-SHADOW still operating out of CORVIUM. Intel: legions are being rotated
off the trench lines, leaves gaps.

RISE, RED AS THE DAWN

I hate this stinking wagon.

The fencer, old Will, burns a candle, as if it can do anything for the
smell. It only makes it hotter in here, more stifling if that's even possible. Besides the stench, though, I feel at ease.

The Stilts is a sleepy village, without much cause for concern. In fact, this happens to be Shade's own birthplace. Not that he talks about home much, other than his sister. I know he writes to them, though. I "mailed" his latest letter myself, leaving it at the post only this morning. Faster than relying on the army to get a letter through, he said, and he was right. Only two or so weeks since he wrote it, rather than the usual month it takes for any kind of Red mail to get anywhere.

"So does this have anything to do with the *new cargo* you've been having my compatriots ferry downriver and overland? To Harbor Bay, yes?" Will glares at me, eyes so bright for someone his age. But his beard looks thinner than it did last month, as is his body. Still, he pours himself a cup of tea with the still hands of a surgeon.

I politely decline the offer of hot tea in an even hotter wagon. *How is he wearing long sleeves?* "What have you heard?"

"This and that."

Wily to the end, these Whistles. "It's true. We're beginning to move people, and the Whistle network has been integral to that operation. I'm hoping you'll agree to join the same."

"Now why would I be stupid enough to do that?"

"Well, you were stupid enough to oath yourself to the Scarlet Guard. But if you need more convincing . . ." With a grin, I pull five silver tetrarchs from my pocket. They barely touch the small table before he snaps them up. They disappear between his fingers. "More for every item."

Still, he does not agree. Putting on a show like the other Whistles did before I eventually won their agreements.

"You would be the first to refuse," I tell him with a slick smile. "And our partnership would cease."

He waves a hand, dismissive. "I do fine without your sort, anyways."

"Is that so?" My smile widens. *Will is no good at bluffing.* "Very well then, I'll go and never darken your . . . wagon again."

Before I can even get up, he stands to stop me. "Who are you planning to move?"

Got you.

"Assets. People who will be valuable to our cause."

As I watch, his bright eyes darken. *A trick of the light.*

"And who makes that decision?"

Despite the heat, a finger of cold runs down my spine. Here comes the usual sticking point. "There are operations all over the country seeking out such people, myself included. We assess, propose our candidates, and wait for approval."

"I assume the old, the sick, and the children set to conscript do not make any of your proposals. No use saving the ones who truly need it."

"If they have valuable skills—"

"Pah!" Will spits, his cheeks going red. He gulps at his tea with angry gasps, draining the cup. The liquid seems to calm him though. When he sets down the empty cup, he rests his chin on his hand thoughtfully. "I suppose that's the best we can hope for."

Another channel opened. "For now."

"Very well."

"Oh, and this most likely won't be a problem here, but I'd stay away from any Silvers you see tomorrow. They won't be happy."

Tomorrow. The thought of it singes my blood. I don't know what the Colonel and Command have planned, only that it includes my broadcast, and something worth waving our flag for.

"Do I want to know?" Will wonders with a pointed smirk. "Do *you* even know?"

I have to laugh openly. "Do you have anything stronger than tea?"

He doesn't get a chance to answer, as someone starts pounding on the wagon door. He jumps, nearly smashing the cup. I catch it deftly, but my eyes are on him. An old tremor of fear shivers through me and we sit still, waiting. Then I remember. *Officers do not knock.*

"Will Whistle!" a girl's voice says. Will all but collapses in relief, and the cord of tension in me releases as well. With one hand, he gestures for me to get behind the curtain dividing his wagon.

I do as asked, hiding myself seconds before she wrenches open the door.

"Miss Barrow!" I hear him say.

A thousand crowns. I curse under my breath as I walk back to the roadside tavern. *Each.* Why I picked such an outrageous number, I can't say. Why I even agreed to see the girl—*Shade's sister, that must have been her*—is less puzzling. But telling her I would help? Save her friend, save *her* from conscription? Two teenagers I don't know, thieves who would most likely get their ferriers killed? But deep down, I know why. I remember the boy in Rocasta, dragged away from his mother. The same happened to Shade and his two older brothers in front of that girl who begged me tonight. *Mare, her name is Mare.* She begged for herself and another, her boyfriend most likely. In her voice, I heard and saw so many people. The Rocastan mother. Rasha, stopping to watch. Tye, dying so close to the place she wanted to escape. Cara, Tarry, Shore, Big Coop. All gone, risking their lives and paying the price the Scarlet Guard always seems to collect.

Not that Mare will come up with the money. It was an impossible task. Still, I owe Shade much and more for his service. I suppose getting his sister away from conscription will be a small price to pay for his intelligence. And whatever she does bring me will go straight to the cause.

Tristan joins me midway between the Stilts and the road tavern.

I half expected him to be all the way there, waiting with Rasha, Little Coop, and Cristobel, the only remaining members of our ill-fated team.

"Successful?" he asks, carefully adjusting his coat to hide the pistol at his hip.

"Very," I respond. The word is surprisingly hard to force out.

Tristan knows me well enough not to pry. Instead, he changes the subject and hands over the Corvium radio. "Barrow's been clicking for the last hour."

Bored again. I don't know how many times I've told Shade the radio is for official business and emergencies, not to annoy me. Still, I can't help but grin. I do my best to keep my lips still, at least in front of Tristan, and start fumbling with the radio.

I click the receiver, sending a pulse of seemingly random dots. *I'm here*, they say.

His response comes so quickly I almost drop the radio.

"Farley, I need out." His voice crackles, tinny through the small speaker. "Farley? I have to get away from Corvium."

Panic spikes down my spine. "Okay," I respond, my mind flying at top speed. "You—you can't get out yourself?" If not for Tristan, I would ask him outright. Why can't he jump himself away from that nightmare fortress?

"Meet me in Rocasta."

"Done."

THE FOLLOWING MESSAGE HAS BEEN DECODED
CONFIDENTIAL, SENIOR CLEARANCE REQUIRED

Day 56 of Operation RED WEB, Stage 2.

Operative: Captain REDACTED.

Designation: LAMB.

Origin: Rocasta, NRT.

Destination: RAM at REDACTED.

-Congratulations on ARCHEON bombing.

-In ROCASTA to remove SHADOW.

RISE, RED AS THE DAWN

THE FOLLOWING MESSAGE HAS BEEN DECODED

CONFIDENTIAL, SENIOR CLEARANCE REQUIRED

Day 60 of Operation SHIELDWALL, Stage 2.

Operative: Colonel REDACTED.

Designation: RAM.

Origin: REDACTED.

Destination: LAMB at Rocasta.

-Proceed. Send him to TRIAL. Return to RED WEB ASAP.

RISE, RED AS THE DAWN.

It took longer to get here than I anticipated. Not to mention the fact that I came alone.

After the bombing in Archeon, travel is difficult, even through our usual channels. Whistle cargo boats and transports are harder to come by. And getting into cities, even Rocasta, is no mean feat. Reds must present identity cards or even their blood at different checkpoints entering the city, checkpoints I must avoid at all cost. Even though my face was masked, hidden in the video during which I announced the presence of the Scarlet Guard to the entire country, I can't take any chances.

I even shaved my head, parting with the long blond braid clearly visible in that broadcast.

Crance, the Mariner working the supply convoy, had to smuggle me in, and it took a great amount of back channeling to get him to agree. Even so, I managed to get into the city proper in one piece, my radio firmly tucked into my waistband.

Red sector. Marketgrove.

That's where Shade wanted to meet, and that's where I must get to. I don't dare cover or hood my face, which would give anyone a better clue as to my identity. Instead, I wear shaded glasses, hiding the one part of my face anyone saw in the video. Still, I feel risk in every step. *Risk is part of the game.* But somehow, my fear isn't for myself. I've done my part, more than my part, for the Scarlet Guard. I could die now and be considered a successful operative. My name would go into someone's correspondence, Tristan's probably, clicked out in dots for the Colonel to read.

I wonder if he would mourn.

It's cloudy today and the mood of the city reflects the weather. And the bombing is on everyone's lips, in everyone's eyes. The Reds are a strange mix of hopeful and downcast, some openly whispering about this so-called Scarlet Guard. But many, the old especially, scowl at their children, scolding them for believing our nonsense, telling them it will bring more trouble to their people. I'm not stupid enough to stop and argue.

Marketgrove is deep in the Red sector, but still crawling with Silver

Security officers. Today they look like wolves on the prowl, their guns in hand rather than holster. I heard news of riots in the major cities, Silver citizens going after any Reds they could get their hands on, blaming everyone they could for the Scarlet Guard's deeds. But something tells me these officers aren't here to protect my people. They only want to instill fear and keep us quiet.

But even they can't stop the whispers.

"Who are they?"

"The Scarlet Guard."

"Never heard of the like."

"Did you see? West Archeon in flames—"

"—but no one was hurt—"

"—they'll bring more trouble—"

"—worse and worse times—"

"—blaming us for it—"

"I want to find them."

"Farley."

The last is a warm breath against the shell of my ear, his voice familiar as my own face. I turn instinctually and pull Shade into a hug, surprising both of us.

"Good to see you too," he mutters.

"Let's get you out of here," I murmur as I pull back. When I look at him properly, I realize the last few weeks have not been kind. His face is pale, his expression drawn, and dark circles ring his eyes. "What happened?"

He tucks my arm in his and I let him lead us through the crowd dutifully walking the market. We look like anyone. "A transfer, to the Storm Legion, to the front."

"Punishment?"

But Shade shakes his head. "Not for passing information. They still don't know I'm the leak or that I'm bleeding everything to the Guard. No, this order is strange."

"Strange how?"

"A general's request. High up. For *me*, an aide. It makes no sense. Just like *something else* doesn't make any sense." His eyes narrow pointedly, and I nod. "I think they know, and I think they're going to get rid of me."

I swallow hard and hope he doesn't notice. My fear for him cannot be construed as anything but professional. "Then we'll execute you first, say you ran off and got shot for deserting. Eastree can falsify the documents like she does with other assets. And besides, it's high time we moved you anyways."

"Do you have any idea where that might be?"

"You'll be going to Trial, across the border. That shouldn't be too difficult for someone with your skills."

"I'm not invincible. I can't jump hundreds of miles, or even, well, *navigate* myself that far. Can you?" he mumbles.

I have to smile. *Crance should work.* "I think I can secure you a map and a guide."

"You're not coming?" I tell myself I'm imagining the disappointment in his voice.

"I have other business to handle first. Careful," I add, noting a cluster of officers up ahead. Shade's arm tightens on mine, pulling me closer. *He'll jump if he has to, and I'll get sick all over my boots again.*

"Try not to make me sick this time," I grumble, drawing his crooked grin.

But there's no need for his trepidation. The officers are focused elsewhere, on a cracked video screen, likely the only one in the Red market. Used for official broadcasts, but there isn't anything official about what they're watching.

"Forgot Queenstrial was today," one of them says, leaning forward to squint at the picture. It blurs occasionally. "Couldn't get a better set for us, eh, Marcos?"

Marcos flushes gray, annoyed. "This is Red sector, what did you expect? You're welcome to go back to rounds if this doesn't satisfy!"

Queenstrial. I remember something about the word. In the briefing on Norta, the packet of cobbled-together information the Colonel made me read before I was sent here. Something about princes—choosing brides, maybe. I wrinkle my nose at the idea, but somehow I can't tear my eyes away from the screen as we get closer and closer.

On it, a girl in black leather demonstrates her storied abilities. *Magnetron*, I realize as she manipulates the metal of whatever arena she's been dropped into.

Then a flash of red drops across the screen, landing hard against the electric shield separating the magnetron girl from the rest of the Silver elite watching her display.

The officers gasp in unison. One of them even turns away. "I don't want to see this," he groans, as if he's about to be sick.

Shade is rooted to the spot, his eyes hard on the screen, watching the red blotch. His grip tightens on me, forcing me to look. *The blotch has a face. His sister.*

Mare Barrow.

He goes cold against me as the lightning swallows her whole.

"It should have killed her."

Shade's hands are shaking and he has to crouch in the alley to keep the rest from following suit. I drop to my knees next to him, one hand on his shivering arm.

"It should have killed her," he says again, his eyes wide and hollow.

I don't need to ask to know he's replaying the scene in his head, over and over again. His young sister falling into the Queenstrial arena. To her death under all circumstances. But Mare didn't die. She was electrocuted on camera, but she didn't die.

"She's alive, Shade," I tell him, turning his face to mine. "You saw yourself, she got up and ran."

"How is that possible?"

Now is not the time to appreciate the joke. "I asked you the same thing once."

"Then she's different too." His eyes darken, sliding away from my face. "And she's with *them*. I have to help her."

He tries to scramble to his feet, but the shock has not worn off. I help him back down as gently as I can, letting him lean on me.

"They'll kill her, Diana," he whispers. His voice breaks my heart. "They could be doing it right now."

"Somehow, I don't think they will. They can't. Not after everyone saw her, a Red girl surviving lightning." *They'll need to explain first. Come up with a story. Just like the stories they used to cover us until we made sure they couldn't anymore.* "She planted a flag of her own today."

Suddenly the alley feels too small. Shade levels a glare, one only a soldier could muster. "I won't leave my sister there alone."

"She won't be. I will make sure of it."

His eyes harden, mirroring the resolve I feel inside.

"So will I."

★ ★ ★

THE FOLLOWING MESSAGE HAS BEEN DECODED
CONFIDENTIAL, COMMAND CLEARANCE REQUIRED

Day 2 of Operation LIGHTNING.
Operative: Captain REDACTED.
Designation: LAMB.
Origin: Summerton, LL.
Destination: COMMAND at REDACTED.

-Op under way. MARE BARROW made contact with WHISTLE WILL and
BONES in ALBANUS, oathed to SG. SHADOW leverage successful.
-Operative MAIDEN will act as her contact within HALL OF THE SUN.
-Operative STEWARD made contact regarding new asset for recruitment
inside HALL OF THE SUN, will explore further.

RISE, RED AS THE DAWN.

Read on for the second book in the
Red Queen series

GLASS SWORD

ONE

I flinch. The rag she gives me is clean, but it still smells like blood. I
shouldn't care. I already have blood all over my clothes. The red is mine,
of course. The silver belongs to many others. Evangeline, Ptolemus,
the nymph lord, all those who tried to kill me in the arena. I suppose
some of it is Cal's as well. He bled freely on the sand, cut and bruised
by our would-be executioners. Now he sits across from me, staring at
his feet, letting his wounds begin the slow process of healing naturally.
I glance at one of the many cuts on my arms, probably from Evangeline. Still fresh, and deep enough to leave a scar. Part of me delights in
the thought. This jagged gash will not be magically wiped away by a
healer's cold hands. Cal and I are not in the Silver world anymore, with
someone to simply erase our well-earned scars. We have escaped. Or at
least, I have. Cal's chains are a firm reminder of his captivity.

Farley nudges my hand, her touch surprisingly gentle. "Hide your
face, lightning girl. It's what they're after."

For once, I do as I'm told. The others follow, pulling red fabric up over their mouths and noses. Cal is the last uncovered face, but not for long. He doesn't fight Farley when she ties his mask into place, making him look like one of us.

If only he was.

An electric hum sets my blood on fire, reminding me of the pulsing, screeching Undertrain. It carries us inexorably forward, to a city that was once a haven. The train races, screaming over ancient tracks like a Silver swift running over open ground. I listen to the grating metal, feel it deep in my bones where a cold ache settles in. My rage, my *strength* back in the arena seem like faraway memories, leaving behind only pain and fear. I can scarcely imagine what Cal must be thinking. He's lost everything, *everything* he ever held dear. A father, a brother, a kingdom. How he's holding himself together, still but for the rocking of the train, I do not know.

No one needs to tell me the reason for our haste. Farley and her Guardsmen, tense as coiled wire, are enough explanation for me. *We are still running.*

Maven came this way before, and Maven will come again. This time with the fury of his soldiers, his mother, and his new crown. Yesterday he was a prince; today he is king. I thought he was my friend, my betrothed, now I know better.

Once, I trusted him. Now I know to hate him, to fear him. He helped kill his father for a crown, and framed his brother for the crime. He knows the radiation surrounding the ruined city is a lie—a trick—and he knows where the train leads. The sanctuary Farley built is no longer safe, not for us. *Not for you.*

We could already be speeding into a trap.

An arm tightens around me, sensing my unease. *Shade.* I still can't believe my brother is here, alive and, strangest of all, like me. Red and Silver—and stronger than both.

"I won't let them take you again," he murmurs, so low I can barely hear him. I suppose loyalty to anyone but the Scarlet Guard, even family, is not allowed. "I promise you that."

His presence is soothing, pulling me backward in time. Past his conscription, to a rainy spring when we could still pretend to be children. Nothing existed but the mud, the village, and our foolish habit of ignoring the future. Now the future is all I think of, wondering what dark path my actions have set us upon.

"What are we going to do now?" I direct the question at Farley, but my eyes find Kilorn. He stands at her shoulder, a dutiful guardian with a clenched jaw and bloody bandages. To think he was a fisherman's apprentice not so long ago. Like Shade, he seems out of place, a ghost of a time before all this.

"There's always somewhere to run," Farley replies, more focused on Cal than anything else.

She expects him to fight, to resist, but he does neither.

"You keep your hands on her," Farley says, turning back to Shade after a long moment. My brother nods, and his palm feels heavy on my shoulder. "She cannot be lost."

I am not a general or a tactician, but her reasoning is clear. I am the little lightning girl—living electricity, a lightning bolt in human form. People know my name, my face, and my abilities. I am valuable, I am powerful, and Maven will do anything to stop me from striking back. How my brother can protect me from the twisted new king, even though he is like me, even though he's the fastest thing I've ever seen, I do not know. But I must believe, even if it seems a miracle. After all, I have seen so many impossible things. Another escape will be the least of them.

The click and slide of gun barrels echo down the train as the Guard makes ready. Kilorn shifts to stand over me, swaying slightly, his grip tight on the rifle slung across his chest. He glances down, his expression soft. He tries to smirk, to make me laugh, but his bright green eyes are grave and afraid.

In contrast, Cal sits quietly, almost peaceful. Though he has the most to fear—chained, surrounded by enemies, hunted by his own brother—he looks serene. I'm not surprised. He's a soldier born and bred. War is something he understands, and we are certainly at war now.

"I hope you don't plan to fight," he says, speaking for the first time in many long minutes. His eyes are on me, but his words bite at Farley. "I hope you plan to run."

"Save your breath, Silver." She squares her shoulders. "I know what we have to do."

I can't stop the words from bursting out. "So does he." The glare she turns on me burns, but I've dealt with worse. I don't even flinch. "Cal knows how they fight, he knows what they'll do to stop us. Use him."

How does it feel to be used? He spit those words at me in the prison beneath the Bowl of Bones and it made me want to die. Now it barely stings.

She doesn't say anything, and that is enough for Cal.

"They'll have Snapdragons," he says grimly.

Kilorn laughs aloud. "Flowers?"

"Airjets," Cal says, his eyes sparking with distaste. "Orange wings, silver bodies, single pilot, easy to maneuver, perfect for an urban assault. They carry four missiles each. Times one squadron, that's forty-eight missiles you're going to have to outrun, plus light ammunition. Can you handle that?"

He's met only with silence. *No, we can't.*

"And the Dragons are the least of our worries. They'll just circle, defend a perimeter, keep us in place until ground troops arrive."

He lowers his eyes, thinking quickly. He's wondering what he would do, if he were on the other side of this. If he were king instead of Maven. "They'll surround us and present terms. Mare and I for your escape."

Another sacrifice. Slowly, I suck in a breath. This morning, yesterday, before all this madness, I would have been glad to give myself over to save just Kilorn and my brother. But now . . . now I know I am special. Now I have others to protect. Now I cannot be lost.

"We can't agree to that," I say. A bitter truth. Kilorn's gaze weighs heavy, but I don't look up. I can't stomach his judgment.

Cal is not so harsh. He nods, agreeing with me. "The king doesn't expect us to give in," he replies. "The jets will bring the ruins down on us, and the rest will mop up the survivors. It will be little more than a massacre."

Farley is a creature of pride, even now when she's terribly cornered. "What do you suggest?" she asks, bending over him. Her words drip disdain. "Total surrender?"

Something like disgust crosses Cal's face. "Maven will still kill you. In a cell or on the battlefield, he won't let any of us live."

"Then better we die fighting." Kilorn's voice sounds stronger than it should, but there's a tremble in his fingers. He looks like the rest of the rebels, willing to do anything for the cause, but my friend is still afraid. Still a boy, no more than eighteen, with too much to live for, and too little reason to die.

Cal scoffs at Kilorn's forced but brazen declaration, yet he doesn't say anything else. He knows a more graphic description of our impending death won't help anyone.

Farley doesn't share his sentiment and waves a hand, dismissing both of them outright. Behind me, my brother mirrors her determination.

They know something we don't, something they won't say yet. Maven has taught us all the price of trust misplaced.

"We are not the ones who die today," is all she says, before marching toward the front of the train. Her boots sound like hammer falls on the metal flooring, each one smacking of stubborn resolve.

I sense the train slow before I feel it. The electricity wanes, weakening, as we glide into the underground station. What we might find in the skies above, white fog or orange-winged airjets, I do not know. The others don't seem to mind, exiting the Undertrain with great purpose. In their silence, the armed and masked Guard looks like true soldiers, but I know better. They're no match for what is coming.

"Prepare yourself." Cal's voice hisses in my ear, making me shiver. It reminds me of days long past, of dancing in moonlight. "Remember how strong you are."

Kilorn shoulders his way to my side, separating us before I can tell Cal my strength and my ability are all I'm sure of now. The electricity in my veins might be the only thing I trust in this world.

I want to believe in the Scarlet Guard, and certainly in Shade and Kilorn, but I won't let myself, not after the mess my trust, my *blindness* toward Maven got us into. And Cal is out of the question altogether. He is a prisoner, a Silver, the enemy who would betray us if he could— if he had anywhere else to run.

But still, somehow, I feel a pull to him. I remember the burdened boy who gave me a silver coin when I was nothing. With that one gesture he changed my future, and destroyed his own.

And we share an alliance—an uneasy one forged in blood and

betrayal. We are connected, we are united—against Maven, against all who deceived us, against the world about to tear itself apart.

Silence waits for us. Gray, damp mist hangs over the ruins of Naercey, bringing the sky down so close I might touch it. It's cold, with the chill of autumn, the season of change and death. Nothing haunts the sky yet, no jets to rain destruction down upon an already destroyed city. Farley sets a brisk pace, leading up from the tracks to the wide, abandoned avenue. The wreckage yawns like a canyon, more gray and broken than I remember.

We march east down the street, toward the shrouded waterfront. The high, half-collapsed structures lean over us, their windows like eyes watching us pass. Silvers could be waiting in the broken hollows and shadowed arches, ready to kill the Scarlet Guard. Maven could make me watch as he struck rebels down one by one. He would not give me the luxury of a clean, quick death. *Or worse*, I think. *He would not let me die at all.*

The thought chills my blood like a Silver shiver's touch. As much as Maven lied to me, I still know a small piece of his heart. I remember him grabbing me through the bars of a cell, holding on with shaking fingers. And I remember the name he carries, the name that reminds me a heart still beats inside him. *His name was Thomas and I watched him die.* He could not save that boy. But he can save me, in his own twisted way.

No. I will never give him the satisfaction of such a thing. I would rather die.

But try as I might, I can't forget the shadow I thought him to be, the lost and forgotten prince. I wish that person were real. I wish he existed somewhere other than my memories.

The Naercey ruins echo strangely, more quiet than they should be. With a start, I realize why. *The refugees are gone.* The woman sweeping mountains of ash, the children hiding in drains, the shadows of my Red brothers and sisters—they have all fled. There's no one left but us.

"Think what you want of Farley, but know she isn't stupid," Shade says, answering my question before I get a chance to ask. "She gave the order to evacuate last night, after she escaped Archeon. She thought you or Maven would talk under torture."

She was wrong. There was no need to torture Maven. He gave his information and his mind freely. He opened his head to his mother, letting her paw through everything she saw there. The Undertrain, the secret city, *the list.* It is all hers now, just like he always was.

The line of Scarlet Guard soldiers stretches out behind us, a disorganized rabble of armed men and women. Kilorn marches directly behind me, his eyes darting, while Farley leads. Two burly soldiers keep Cal on her heels, gripping his arms tensely. With their red scarves, they look like the stuff of nightmares. But there are so few of us now, maybe thirty, all walking wounded. So few survived.

"There's not enough of us to keep this rebellion going, even if we escape again," I whisper to my brother. The low-hanging mist muffles my voice, but he still hears me.

The corner of his mouth twitches, wanting to smile. "That's not your concern."

Before I can press him, the soldier in front of us halts. He is not the only one. At the head of the line, Farley holds up a fist, glaring at the slate-gray sky. The rest mirror her, searching for what we cannot see. Only Cal keeps his eyes on the ground. He already knows what our doom looks like.

A distant, inhuman scream reaches down through the mist. This sound is mechanical and constant, circling overhead. And it is not alone. Twelve arrow-shaped shadows race through the sky, their orange wings cutting in and out of the clouds. I've never seen an airjet properly, not so close or without the cover of night, so I can't stop my jaw from dropping when they come into view. Farley barks orders at the Guard, but I don't hear her. I'm too busy staring at the sky, watching winged death arc overhead. Like Cal's cycle, the flying machines are beautiful, impossibly curved steel and glass. I suppose a magnetron had something to do with their construction—how else can metal *fly*? Blue-tinged engines spark beneath their wings, the telltale sign of electricity. I can barely feel the twinge of them, like a breath against skin, but they're too far away for me to affect. I can only watch—in horror.

They screech and twist around the island of Naercey, never breaking their circle. I can almost pretend they're harmless, nothing but curious birds come to see the obliterated remnants of a rebellion. Then a dart of gray metal sails overhead, trailing smoke, moving almost too fast to see. It collides with a building down the avenue, disappearing through a broken window. A bloom of red-orange explodes a split second later, destroying the entire floor of an already crumbling building. It shatters in on itself, collapsing onto thousand-year-old supports that snap like toothpicks. The entire structure tips, falling so slowly the sight can't be real. When it hits the street, blockading the way ahead of us, I feel the rumble deep in my chest. A cloud of smoke and dust hits us head-on, but I don't cower. It takes more than that to scare me now.

Through the gray-and-brown haze, Cal stands with me, even while his captors crouch. Our eyes meet for a moment, and his shoulders droop. It's the only sign of defeat he'll let me see.

Farley grabs the nearest Guardsman, hoisting her to her feet. "Scatter!" she shouts, gesturing to the alleys on either side of us. "To the north side, to the tunnels!" She points to her lieutenants as she speaks, telling them where to go. "Shade, to the park side!" My brother nods, knowing what she means. Another missile careens into a nearby building, drowning her out. But it's easy to tell what she's shouting.

Run.

Part of me wants to hold my ground, to stand, to fight. My purple-and-white lightning will certainly make me a target and draw the jets away from the fleeing Guard. I might even take a plane or two with me. But that cannot be. I'm worth more than the rest, more than red masks and bandages. Shade and I must survive—if not for the cause, then for the others. For the list of hundreds like us—hybrids, anomalies, freaks, Red-and-Silver impossibilities—who will surely die if we fail.

Shade knows this as well as I do. He loops his arm into mine, his grip so tight as to be bruising. It's almost too easy to run in step with him, to let him guide me off the wide avenue and into a gray-green tangle of overgrown trees spilling into the street. The deeper we go, the thicker they become, gnarled together like deformed fingers. A thousand years of neglect turned this little plot into a dead jungle. It shelters us from the sky, until we can only hear the jets circling closer and closer. Kilorn is never far behind. For a moment, I can pretend we're back at home, wandering the Stilts, looking for fun and trouble.

Trouble is all we seem to find.

When Shade finally skids to a stop, his heels scarring the dirt beneath us, I chance a glance around. Kilorn halts next to us, his rifle aimed uselessly skyward, but no one else follows. I can't even see the street anymore, or the red rags fleeing into the ruins.

My brother glares up through the boughs of the trees, watching and waiting for the jets to fly out of range.

"Where are we going?" I ask him, breathless.

Kilorn answers instead. "The river," he says. "And then the ocean. Can you take us?" He glances at Shade's hands, as if he could see his ability plain in his flesh. But Shade's strength is buried like mine, invisible until he chooses to reveal it.

My brother shakes his head. "Not in one jump, it's too far. And I'd rather run, save my strength." His eyes darken. "Until we really need it."

I nod, agreeing. I know firsthand what it is to be ability-worn, tired in your bones, barely able to move, let alone fight.

"Where are they taking Cal?"

My question makes Kilorn wince.

"Hell if I care."

"You should," I fire back, even as my voice shakes with hesitation. *No, he shouldn't. Neither should you. If the prince is gone, you must let him go.* "He can help us get out of this. He can fight *with* us."

"He'll escape or kill us the second we give him the chance," he snaps, tearing away his scarf to show the angry scowl beneath.

In my head, I see Cal's fire. It burns everything in its path, from metal to flesh. "He could've killed you already," I say. It's not an exaggeration, and Kilorn knows it.

"Somehow I thought you two would outgrow your bickering," Shade says, stepping between us. "How silly of me."

Kilorn forces out an apology through gritted teeth, but I do no such thing. My focus is on the jets, letting their electric hearts beat against mine. They weaken with each second, getting farther and farther away. "They're flying away from us. If we're going to go, we need to do it now."

Both my brother and Kilorn look at me strangely, but neither argue.

"This way," Shade says, pointing through the trees. A small, almost invisible path winds through them, where the dirt has been swept away to reveal stone and asphalt beneath. Again, Shade links his arm through mine, and Kilorn charges ahead, setting a swift pace for us to follow.

Branches scrape against us, bending over the narrowing path, until it's impossible for us to run side by side. But instead of letting me go, Shade squeezes even tighter. And then I realize he's not squeezing me at all. It's the air, the *world*. Everything and anything tightens in a blistering, black second. And then, in a blink, we're on the other side of the trees, looking back to see Kilorn emerge from the gray grove.

"But he was ahead," I murmur aloud, looking back and forth between Shade and the pathway. We cross into the middle of the street, with the sky and smoke drifting overhead. "You—"

Shade grins. The action seems out of place against the distant scream of jets. "Let's say I . . . jumped. As long as you're holding on to me, you'll be able to come along," he says, before hurrying us into the next alley.

My heart races with the knowledge that I just *teleported*, to the point where it's almost possible to forget our predicament.

The jets are quick to remind me. Another missile explodes to the north, bringing down a building with the rumble of an earthquake. Dust races down the alley in a wave, painting us in another layer of gray. Smoke and fire are so familiar to me now that I barely smell it, even when ash begins to fall like snow. We leave our footprints in it. Perhaps they will be the last marks we make.

Shade knows where to go and how to run. Kilorn has no trouble keeping up, even with the rifle weighing him down. By now, we've circled back to the avenue. To the east, a swirl of daylight breaks through the dirt and dust, bringing with it a salty gasp of sea air. To the west, the first collapsed building lies like a fallen giant, blocking any retreat to the train. Broken glass, the iron skeletons of buildings, and strange slabs of faded white screens rise around us, a palace of ruins.

What was this? I dimly wonder. *Julian would know.* Just thinking his name hurts, and I push the sensation away.

A few other red rags dart through the ashen air, and I look for a familiar silhouette. But Cal is nowhere to be seen, and it makes me so terribly afraid.

"I'm not leaving without him."

Shade doesn't bother to ask who I'm talking about. He already knows.

"The prince is coming with us. I give you my word."

My response cuts my insides. "I don't trust your word."

Shade is a soldier. His life has been anything but easy, and he is no stranger to pain. Still, my declaration wounds him deeply. I see it in his face.

I'll apologize later, I tell myself.

If later ever comes.

Another missile sails overhead, striking a few streets away. The distant thunder of an explosion doesn't mask the harsher and more terrifying noise rising all around.

The rhythm of a thousand marching feet.

TWO

The air thickens with a cloak of ash, buying us a few seconds to stare down our oncoming doom. The silhouettes of soldiers move down the streets from the north. I can't see their guns yet, but a Silver army doesn't need guns to kill.

Other Guardsmen flee before us, sprinting down the avenue with abandon. For now, it looks like they might escape, but to where? There's only the river and the sea beyond. There's nowhere to go, nowhere to hide. The army marches slowly, at a strange shuffling pace. I squint through the dust, straining to see them. And then I realize what this is, what Maven has done. The shock of it sparks in me, *through* me, forcing Shade and Kilorn to jump back.

"Mare!" Shade shouts, half-surprised, half-angry. Kilorn doesn't say anything, watching me wobble on the spot.

My hand closes on his arm and he doesn't flinch. My sparks are already gone—he knows I won't hurt him. "Look," I say, pointing.

We knew soldiers would come. Cal told us, *warned us*, that Maven would send in a legion after the airjets. But not even Cal could have predicted this. Only a heart so twisted as Maven's could dream up this nightmare.

The figures of the first line are not wearing the clouded gray of Cal's hard-trained Silver soldiers. They are not even soldiers at all. They are servants in red coats, red shawls, red tunics, red pants, red shoes. So much red they could be bleeding. And around their feet, clinking against the ground, are iron chains. The sound scrapes against me, drowning out the airjets and the missiles and even the harsh-barked orders of the Silver officers hiding behind their Red wall. The chains are all I hear.

Kilorn bristles, growling. He steps forward, raising his rifle to shoot, but the gun shudders in his hands. The army is still across the avenue, too far for an expert shot even *without* a human shield. Now it's worse than impossible.

"We have to keep moving," Shade mutters. Anger flares in his eyes, but he knows what must be done, what must be *ignored*, to stay alive. "Kilorn, come with us now, or we'll leave you."

My brother's words sting, waking me up from my horrified daze. When Kilorn doesn't move, I take his arm, whispering into his ear, hoping to drown out the chains.

"Kilorn." It's the voice I used on Mom when my brothers went to war, when Dad had a breathing attack, when things fell apart. "Kilorn, there's nothing we can do for them."

The words hiss through his teeth. "That's not true." He glances over his shoulder at me. "You have to do *something*. You can save them—"

To my eternal shame, I shake my head. "No, I can't."

We keep running. And Kilorn follows.

More missiles explode, faster and closer with each passing second. I can barely hear over the ringing in my ears. Steel and glass sway like reeds in the wind, bending and breaking until biting silver rain falls down upon us. Soon, it's too dangerous to run, and Shade's grip tightens on me. He grabs Kilorn too, jumping all three of us as the world collapses. My stomach twists every time the darkness closes in, and every time, the falling city gets closer. Ash and concrete dust choke our vision, making it difficult to breathe. Glass shatters in a bright storm, leaving shallow cuts across my face and hands, shredding my clothes. Kilorn looks worse than I do, his bandages red with fresh blood, but he keeps moving, careful not to outpace us. My brother's grip never weakens, but he begins to tire, paling with every new jump. I'm not helpless, using my sparks to deflect the jagged metal shrapnel that even Shade can't jump us away from. But we're not enough, not even to save ourselves.

"How much farther?" My voice sounds small, drowned out by the tide of war. Against the haze, I can't see farther than a few feet. But I can still *feel*. And what I feel are wings, engines, *electricity* screaming overhead, swooping closer and closer. We might as well be mice waiting for hawks to pluck us from the ground.

Shade stops us short, his honey-colored eyes sweeping back and forth. For one frightening second, I fear he might be lost. "Wait," he says, knowing something we don't.

He stares upward, at the skeleton of a once great structure. It's massive, taller than the highest spire of the Hall of the Sun, wider than the great Caesar's Square of Archeon. A tremor runs down my spine when I realize—it's *moving*. Back and forth, side to side, swaying on twisting supports already worn by centuries of neglect. As we watch, it starts to tip, slumping slowly at first, like an old man settling into his chair. Then faster and faster, falling above us and around us.

"Hold on to me," Shade shouts over the din, adjusting his grip on us both. He wraps his arm around my shoulders, crushing me to him, almost too tight to bear. I expect the now unpleasant sensation of jumping, but it never comes. Instead, I'm greeted by a more familiar sound.

Gunfire.

Now it isn't Shade's ability saving my life, but his flesh. A bullet meant for me catches him in the meat of his upper arm, while another strafes his leg. He roars in anguish, almost falling to the cracked earth beneath. I feel the shot through him, but I have no time for pain. More bullets sing through the air, too fast and numerous to fight. We can only run, fleeing both the collapsing building and the oncoming army. One cancels out the other, with the twisted steel falling between the legion and us. At least, that's what should happen. Gravity and fire made the structure fall, but the might of magnetrons stop it from shielding us. When I look back, I can see them, with silver hair and black armor, a dozen or so sweeping away every falling beam and steel support. I'm not close enough to see their faces, but I know House Samos well enough. Evangeline and Ptolemus direct their family, clearing the street so the legion can press on. So they can finish what they started and kill us all.

If only Cal had destroyed Ptolemus in the arena; if only I had shown Evangeline the same level of kindness she showed me. Then we might have a chance. But our mercy has a cost, and it might be our lives.

I hold on to my brother, supporting him as best I can. Kilorn does most of the heavy lifting. He takes the bulk of Shade's weight, half dragging him toward a still smoking impact crater. We gladly dive into it, finding some refuge from the storm of bullets. But not much. Not for long.

Kilorn pants and sweat beads on his brow. He rips off one of his own sleeves, using it to bandage up Shade's leg. Blood stains it quickly. "Can you jump?"

My brother furrows his brow, feeling not his pain but his strength. I understand that well enough. Slowly he shakes his head, his eyes going dark. "Not yet."

Kilorn curses under his breath. "Then what do we do?"

It takes me a second to realize he's asking me and not my older brother. Not the soldier who knows battle better than us. But he's not really asking me either. Not Mare Barrow of the Stilts, the thief, his friend. Kilorn is looking to someone else now, to who I became in the halls of a palace and the sands of an arena.

He's asking the lightning girl.

"Mare, what do we do?"

"You leave me, that's what you do!" Shade growls through clenched teeth, answering before I can. "You run to the river, you find Farley. I'll jump to you as soon as I can."

"Don't lie to a liar," I say, trying my best to keep from shaking. My brother was only just returned to me, a ghost back from the dead. I won't let him slip away again, not for anything. "We're getting out of here together. *All* of us."

The legion's march rumbles the ground. One glance over the edge of the crater tells me they're less than a hundred yards away, advancing fast. I can see the Silvers between the gaps in the Red line. The foot soldiers wear the clouded gray uniforms of the army, but some have armor, the plates chased with familiar colors. Warriors from the High Houses. I see bits of blue, yellow, black, brown, and more. Nymphs and telkies and silks and strongarms, the most powerful fighters the Silvers can throw at us. They think Cal the king's killer, me a terrorist, and they'll bring the whole city down to destroy us.

Cal.

Only my brother's blood and Kilorn's uneven breathing keeps me from vaulting out of the crater. I must find him, I *must*. If not for myself then for the cause, to protect the retreat. He's worth a hundred good soldiers. He's a golden shield. But he's probably gone, escaped, having melted his chains and run when the city began to crumble.

No, he wouldn't run. He would never run from that army, from Maven, or from me.

I hope I'm not wrong.

I hope he isn't already dead.

"Get him up, Kilorn." In the Hall of the Sun, the late Lady Blonos taught me how to speak like a princess. It is a cold voice, unyielding, leaving no room for contest.

Kilorn obeys, but Shade still has it in him to protest. "I'll only slow you down."

"You can apologize for that later," I reply, helping him hop to his feet. But I'm barely paying attention to them, my concentration elsewhere. "Get moving."

"Mare, if you think we're leaving you—"

When I turn on Kilorn, I have sparks in my hands and determination in my heart. His words die on his lips. He glances past me, toward the army advancing with every passing second. Telkies and magnetrons scrape debris out of the street, opening the obliterated way with resounding scrapes of metal on stone.

"Run."

Again, he obeys and Shade can do nothing but limp along, leaving me behind. As they clamber out of the crater, scrambling west, I take measured steps east. The army will stop for me. They must.

After one terrifying second, the Reds slow, their chains clinking as they halt. Behind them, Silvers balance black rifles on their shoulders, as if they were nothing at all. The war transports, great machines with treaded wheels, grind to a screeching stop somewhere behind the army. I can feel their power thrum through my veins.

The army is close enough now that I hear officers bark orders. "The lightning girl!" "Keep the line, stand firm!" "Take aim!" "Hold your fire!"

The worst comes last, ringing out against the suddenly quiet street. Ptolemus's voice is familiar, full of hatred and rage.

"Make way for the king!" he shouts.

I stagger back. I expected Maven's armies, but not Maven himself. He is not a soldier like his brother, and he has no business leading an army. But here he is, stalking through the parting troops, with Ptolemus and Evangeline on his heels. When he steps out from behind the Red line, my knees almost buckle. His armor is polished black, his cape crimson. Somehow he seems taller than he did this morning. He still wears his father's crown of flames, though it has no place on a battlefield. I suppose he wants to show the world what he's won with his lies, what a great prize he's stolen. Even from so far away, I can feel the heat of his glare and his roiling anger. It burns me from inside out.

Nothing but the jets whistle overhead; it is the only sound in the world.

"I see you're still brave," Maven says, his voice carrying down the avenue. It echoes among the ruins, taunting me. "And foolish."

Like in the arena, I will not give him the satisfaction of my anger and fear.

"They should call you the little quiet girl." He laughs coldly, and his army laughs with him. The Reds remain silent, their eyes fixed on the ground. They don't want to watch what's about to happen. "Well, quiet girl, tell your rat friends it is over. They are surrounded. Call them out, and I will give them the gift of good deaths."

Even if I could give such an order, I never would. "They're already gone."

Don't lie to a liar, and Maven is the grandest liar of all.

Still, he looks unsure. The Scarlet Guard has escaped so many times already, in Caesar's Square, in Archeon. Perhaps they might escape even now. What an embarrassment that would be. What a disastrous start to his reign.

"And the traitor?" His voice sharpens, and Evangeline moves closer to him. Her silver hair glints like the edge of a razor, brighter than her gilded armor. But he moves away from her, batting her aside like a cat would a toy. "What about my wretched brother, the fallen prince?"

He never hears my answer, for I have none.

Maven laughs again and this time it stabs through my heart. "Has he abandoned you too? Did he run away? The coward kills our father and tries to steal my throne, only to slink off and hide?" He bristles, pretending for the sake of his nobles and soldiers. For them, he must still seem the tragic son, a king never meant for a crown, who wants nothing more than justice for the dead.

I raise my chin in challenge. "Do you think Cal would do such a thing?"

Maven is far from foolish. He is wicked but not stupid, and he knows his brother better than anyone else alive. Cal is no coward and never will be. Lying to his subjects will never change that. Maven's eyes betray his heart and he glances sidelong, at the alleys and streets leading away from the war-torn avenue. Cal could be hiding in any one, waiting to strike. I could even be the trap, the bait to draw out the weasel I once called my betrothed and my friend. When he turns his head, his crown slips, too big for his skull. Even the metal knows it does not belong to him.

"I think you stand alone, Mare." He speaks softly. Despite all he's done to me, my name in his mouth makes me shiver, thinking of days gone by. Once he said it with kindness and affection. Now it sounds like a curse. "Your friends are gone. You have lost. And you are an abomination, the only one of your wretched kind. It will be a mercy to remove you from this world."

More lies, and we both know it. I mirror his cold laugh. For a second, we look like friends again. Nothing is further from the truth.

A jet overhead sweeps by, its wings almost scraping the tip of a nearby ruin. It's so close. *Too close.* I can feel its electric heart, its whirring engines somehow keeping it aloft. I reach for it as best I can, like I have so many times before. Like the lights, like the cameras, like every wire and circuit since I became the lightning girl, I take hold of it—and *shut it off.*

The airjet dips, nose down, gliding for a moment on heavy wings. Its original trajectory meant to take it above the avenue, high over the legion to protect the king. Now it dives headfirst into them, sailing over the Red line to collide with hundreds of Silvers. The Samos magnetrons and Provos telkies aren't quick enough to stop the jet as it plows into the street, sending asphalt and bodies flying. The resounding boom as it explodes nearly knocks me off my feet, pushing me farther away. The blast is deafening, disorienting, and painful. *No time for pain* repeats in my head. I don't bother to watch the chaos of Maven's army. I am already running, and my lightning is with me.

Purple-and-white sparks shield my back, keeping me safe from the swifts trying to run me down. A few collide with my lightning, trying to break through. They fall back in piles of smoked flesh and twitching bone. I'm grateful I can't see their faces, or else I might dream of them later. Bullets come next, but my zigzagging sprint makes me a difficult target. The few shots that get close shriek apart in my shield, like my body was supposed to when I fell into the electric net at Queenstrial. That moment seems so long ago. Overhead, the jets scream again, this time careful to keep their distance. Their missiles are not so polite.

The ruins of Naercey stood for thousands of years, but will not survive this day. Buildings and streets crumble, destroyed by Silver powers and missiles alike. Everything and everyone has been unleashed. The magnetrons twist and snap steel support beams, while telkies and strongarms hurl rubble through the ashen sky. Water bleeds up from the sewers as nymphs attempt to flood the city, flushing out the last of the Guardsmen hiding in the tunnels below us. The wind howls, strong as a hurricane, from the windweavers in the army. Water and rubble sting my eyes, the gusts so sharp they are nearly blinding. Oblivions' explosions rock the ground beneath me and I stumble, confused. I never used to fall. But now my face scrapes against the asphalt, leaving blood in my wake. When I get back up, a banshee's glass-shattering scream knocks me down again, forcing me to cover my ears. More blood there, dripping fast and thick between my fingers. But the banshee who flattened me has accidentally saved me. As I fall, another missile blasts over my head, so near I feel it ripple the air.

It explodes too close, the heat pulsing through my hasty lightning shield. Dimly, I wonder if I'll die without eyebrows. But instead of burning through me, the heat stands constant, uncomfortable but not unbearable. Strong, bruising hands wrench me to my feet, and blond hair glints in the firelight. I can just make out her face through the biting windstorm. *Farley*. Her gun is gone, her clothes torn, and her muscles quiver, but she keeps holding me up.

Behind her, a tall, familiar figure cuts a black silhouette against the explosion. He holds it back with a single, outstretched hand. His shackles are gone, melted or cast away. When he turns, the flames grow, licking at the sky and the destroyed street, but never us. Cal knows exactly what he's doing, directing the firestorm around us like water around rock. As in the arena, he forms a burning wall across the avenue, protecting us from his brother and the legion beyond. But now, his flames are strong, fed by oxygen and rage. They leap up into the air, so hot the base burns ghostly blue.

More missiles drop, but again, Cal contains their power, using it to feed his own. It's almost beautiful, watching his long arms arc and turn, transforming destruction into protection with steady rhythm.

Farley tries to pull me away, overpowering me. With the flames defending us, I turn to see the river a hundred yards away. I can even see the hulking shadows of Kilorn and my brother, limping toward supposed safety.

"Come on, Mare," she growls, half dragging my bruised and weakened body.

For a second, I let her pull me along. It hurts too much to think clearly. But one glance back and I understand what she's doing, what she's trying to make *me* do.

"I'm not leaving without him!" I shout for the second time today.

"I think he's doing fine on his own," she says, her blue eyes reflecting the fire.

Once, I thought like her. That Silvers were invincible, gods upon the earth, too powerful to destroy. But I killed three just this morning; Arven, the Rhambos strongarm, and the nymph lord Osanos. Probably more with the lightning storm. And they almost killed me, and Cal, for that matter. We had to save each other in the arena. And we must do so again.

Farley is bigger than me, taller and stronger, but I'm more agile. Even banged up and half-deaf. One flick of my ankle, one well-timed shove, and she stumbles backward, letting go. I turn in the same motion, palms outstretched, feeling for what I need. Naercey has far less electricity than Archeon or even the Stilts, but I don't need to leach power from anything now. I make my own.

The first blast of nymph water pounds against the flames with the strength of a tidal wave. Most of it flash boils into vapor, but the rest falls on the wall, extinguishing the great tongues of fire. I answer the water with my own electricity, aiming for the waves curling and crashing in midair. Behind the wave, the Silver legion marches forward, lunging for us. At least the chained Reds have been pulled away, relegated to the back of the line. Maven's doing. He won't let them slow him down.

His soldiers meet my lightning instead of open air, and behind it, Cal's fire jumps back up from the embers.

"Move back slowly," Cal says, gesturing with an open hand. I mirror his measured steps, careful not to look away from the oncoming doom. Together we alternate back and forth, protecting our own retreat. When his flame falls, my lightning rises, and so on. Together, we have a chance.

He mutters little commands: when to step, when to raise a wall, when to let it drop. He looks more exhausted than I've ever seen him, his veins blue-black beneath pale skin, with gray circles rimming his eyes. I know I must look worse. But his pacing keeps us from giving out entirely, allowing little bits of our strengths to return just when we need.

"Just a little farther," Farley calls, her voice echoing from behind. But she's not running off. She's staying with us, even though she's just human. *She's braver than I gave her credit for.*

"Farther to what?" I growl through gritted teeth, tossing up another net of electricity. Despite Cal's commands, I'm getting slower, and a bit of rubble flies through. It breaks a few yards away, crumbling into dust. We are running out of time.

But so is Maven.

I can smell the river, and the ocean beyond. Sharp and salty, it beckons, but to what end, I have no idea. I only know that Farley and Shade believe it will save us from Maven's jaws. When I glance behind me, I see nothing but the avenue, dead-ending at the river's edge. Farley stands, waiting, her short hair stirring in the hot wind. *Jump*, she mouths, before plunging off the edge of the crumbled street.

What is it with her and leaping into an abyss?

"She wants us to jump," I tell Cal, turning back just in time to supplant his wall.

He grunts in agreement, too focused to speak. Like my lightning, his fires grow weak and thin. We can almost see through them now, to the soldiers on the other side. Flickering flame distorts their features, turning eyes into burning coals, mouths into smiling fangs, and men into demons.

One of them steps up to the wall of fire, close enough to burn. But he doesn't. Instead, he draws the flames apart like a curtain.

Only one person can do that.

Maven shakes embers from his silly cape, letting the silk burn away while his armor holds firm. He has the gall to smile.

And somehow, Cal has the strength to turn away. Instead of tearing Maven apart with his bare hands, he takes my wrist in his searing-hot grip. We sprint together, not bothering to defend our backs. Maven is no match for either of us, and he knows it. Instead, he screams. Despite the crown and the blood on his hands, he is still so young.

"Run, murderer! Run, lightning girl! Run fast and far!" His laughter echoes off the crumbling ruins, haunting me. "There is nowhere I won't find you!"

I'm dimly aware of my lightning failing, giving out as I get farther away. Cal's own flame crumbles with it, exposing us to the rest of the legion. But we're already jumping through midair, to the river ten feet below.

We land, not with a splash but the resounding clang of metal. I have to roll to keep from shattering my ankles, but still feel a hollow, aching pain run up my bones. *What?* Farley waits, knee-deep in the cold river, next to a cylindrical metal tube with an open top. Without speaking she clambers into it, disappearing into whatever lies beneath us. We have no time to argue or ask questions, and follow blindly.

At least Cal has the good sense to close the tube behind us, shutting out the river and the war above. It hisses pneumatically, forming an airtight seal. But that won't protect us for long, not against the legion.

"More tunnels?" I ask breathlessly, whirling to Farley. My vision spots with the motion and I have to slump against the wall, my legs shaking.

Like she did on the street, Farley puts one arm under my shoulder, supporting my weight. "No, this isn't a tunnel," she says with a puzzling smirk.

And then I feel it. Like a battery humming somewhere, but bigger. Stronger. It pulses all around us, down the strange hallway swimming with blinking buttons and low, yellow lights. I glimpse red scarves moving down the passage, hiding the faces of the Guardsmen. They look hazy, like crimson shadows. With a groan, the whole hall shudders and *drops*, angling downward. *Into the water.*

"A boat. An underwater boat," Cal says. His voice is faraway, shaky, and weak. Just like I feel.

Neither of us makes it more than a few feet before we collapse against the sloping walls.

THREE

In the past few days, I've woken up in a jail cell and then on a train. Now it's an underwater boat. *Where will I wake up tomorrow?*

I'm beginning to think this has all been a dream, or a hallucination, or worse. But can you feel tired in dreams? Because I certainly do. My exhaustion is bone-deep, in every muscle and nerve. My heart is another wound entirely, still bleeding from betrayal and failure. When I open my eyes, finding cramped, gray walls, everything I want to forget comes rushing back. It's like Queen Elara is in my head again, forcing me to relive my worst memories. As much as I try, I can't stop them.

My quiet maids were executed, guilty of nothing but painting my skin. Tristan, speared like a pig. Walsh. She was my brother's age, a servant from the Stilts, my friend—*one of us.* And she died cruelly, by her own hand, to protect the Guard, our purpose, and me. Even more died in the tunnels of Caesar's Square, Guardsmen killed by Cal's soldiers, killed by our foolish plan. The memory of red blood burns, but so does the thought of silver. Lucas, a friend, a protector, a Silver with a kind heart, executed for what Julian and I made him do. Lady Blonos, decapitated because she taught me how to sit properly. Colonel Macanthos, Reynald Iral, Belicos Lerolan. Sacrificed for the cause. I almost retch when I remember Lerolan's twin boys, four years old, killed in the explosion that followed the shooting. Maven told me it was an accident—a punctured gas line, but now I know better. His evil runs too deep for such coincidence. I doubt he minded throwing a few more bodies on the blaze, if only to convince the world the Guard was made of monsters. He'll kill Julian too, and Sara. They're probably dead already. I can't think of them at all. It's too painful. Now my thoughts turn back to Maven himself, to cold blue eyes and the moment I realized his charming smile hid a beast.

The bunk beneath me is hard, the blankets thin, with no pillow to speak of, but part of me wants to lie back down. Already my headache returns, throbbing with the electric pulse of this miracle boat. It is a firm reminder—there is no peace for me here. Not yet, not while so much more must be done. *The list. The names. I must find them. I must keep them safe from Maven and his mother.* Heat spreads across my face, my skin flushing with the memory of Julian's little book of hard-won secrets. A record of those like me, with the strange mutation that gives us Red blood and Silver abilities. The list is Julian's legacy. And mine.

I swing my legs over the side of the cot, almost thwacking my head on the bunk above me, and find a neatly folded set of clothing on the floor. Black pants that are too long, a dark red shirt with threadbare elbows, and boots missing laces. Nothing like the fine clothes I found in a Silver cell, but they feel right against my skin.

I barely have the shirt over my head when my compartment door bangs open on great iron hinges. Kilorn waits expectantly on the other side, his smile forced and grim. He shouldn't blush, having seen me in various stages of undress for many summers, but his cheeks redden anyway.

"It's not like you to sleep so long," he says, and I hear worry in his voice.

I shrug it off and stand on weak legs. "I guess I needed it." An odd ringing in my ears takes hold, piercing but not painful. I shake my head back and forth, trying to get rid of it, looking like a wet dog in the process.

"That'll be the banshee scream." He crosses to me and takes my head in gentle but callused hands. I submit to his examination, sighing in annoyance. He turns me sideways, glancing at ears that ran red with blood however long ago. "You're lucky it didn't hit you head-on."

"I'm a lot of things, but I don't think lucky is one of them."

"You're alive, Mare," he says sharply, pulling away. "That's more than many can say." His glare brings me back to Naercey, when I told my brother I didn't trust his word. Deep in my heart, I know I still don't.

"I'm sorry," I mutter quickly. Of course I know others have died, for the cause and for me. But I've died too. Mare of the Stilts died the day she fell onto a lightning shield. Mareena, the lost Silver princess, died in the Bowl of Bones. And I don't know what new person opened her eyes on the Undertrain. I only know what she has been and what she has lost, and the weight of it is almost crushing.

"Are you going to tell me where we're going, or is that another secret?" I try to keep the bitterness from my voice but fail miserably.

Kilorn is polite enough to ignore it and leans back against the door. "We left Naercey five hours ago, and we're headed northeast. That's honestly all I know."

"And that doesn't bother you at all?"

He only shrugs. "What makes you think the higher-ups trust me, or you, for that matter? You know better than anyone how foolish we've been, and the high cost we've paid." Again, I feel the sting of memory. "You said yourself, you can't even trust Shade. I doubt anyone's going to be sharing secrets anytime soon."

The jab doesn't hurt as much as I expected it to. "How is he?"

Kilorn tosses his head, gesturing out to the hallway. "Farley carved out a nice little medical station for the wounded. He's doing better than the others. Cursing a lot, but definitely better." His green eyes darken a bit, and he turns his gaze away. "His leg—"

I draw in a startled breath. "Infected?" At home in the Stilts, infection was as bad as a severed arm. We didn't have much medicine, and once the blood went bad, all you could do was keep chopping, hoping to outrun fever and blackened veins.

To my relief, Kilorn shakes his head. "No, Farley dosed him good, and the Silvers fight with clean bullets. So that's big of them." He laughs darkly, expecting me to join him. Instead, I shiver. The air is so cold down here. "But he'll definitely be limping for a while."

"Will you take me to him or do I have to figure out the way myself?"

Another dark laugh and he extends his arm. To my surprise, I find that I need his support to help me walk. Naercey and the Bowl of Bones have certainly taken their toll.

Mersive. That's what Kilorn calls the strange underwater boat. How it manages to sail *beneath* the ocean is beyond both of us, though I'm sure Cal will figure it out. He's next on my list. I'll find him after I make sure my brother is still breathing. I remember Cal being barely conscious when we escaped, just like me. But I don't suppose Farley will set him up in the medical station, not with injured Guardsmen all around. There's too much bad blood and no one wants an inferno in a sealed metal tube.

The banshee's scream still rings in my head, a dull whine that I try to ignore. And with every step, I learn about new aches and bruises. Kilorn notes my every wince and slows his pace, allowing me to lean on his arm. He ignores his own wounds, deep cuts hidden beneath yet another set of fresh bandages. He always had battered hands, bruised and cut from fishing hooks and rope, but they were familiar wounds. They meant he was safe, employed, free from conscription. If not for one dead fish master, little scars would be his only burden.

Once that thought would have made me sad. Now I feel only rage.

The main passage of the mersive is long but narrow, divided by several metal doors with thick hinges and pressurized seals. To close off portions if need be, to stop the entire vessel from flooding and sinking. But the doors give me no comfort whatsoever. I can't stop thinking about dying at the bottom of the ocean, locked in a watery coffin. Even Kilorn, a boy raised on water, seems uncomfortable. The dim lights set into the ceiling filter strangely, cutting shadows across his face to make him appear old and drawn.

The other Guardsmen aren't so affected, coming and going with great purpose. Their red scarves and shawls have been lowered, revealing faces set in grim determination. They carry charts, trays of medical supplies, bandages, food, or even the occasional rifle down the passage, always hurrying and chattering to each other. But they stop at the sight of me, pressing back against the walls to give me as much room as possible in the narrow space. The more daring ones look me in the eye, watching me limp past, but most stare at their feet.

A few even seem afraid.

Of me.

I want to say thank you, to somehow express how deeply indebted I am to every man and woman aboard this strange ship. *Thank you for your service* almost slips past my lips, but I clench my jaw to keep it back. *Thank you for your service.* It's what they print in the notices, the letters sent to tell you your children have died for a useless war. How many parents did I watch weep over those words? How many more will receive them, when the Measures send even younger children to the front?

None, I tell myself. *Farley will have a plan for that, just like we will come up with a way to find the newbloods—the others like me. We will do something. We must do something.*

The Guardsmen against the wall mutter among themselves as I pass. Even the ones who can't stand to look at me whisper to one another, not bothering to mask their words. I suppose they think what they're saying is a compliment.

"The lightning girl" echoes from them, bouncing off the metal walls. It surrounds me like Elara's wretched whispers, ghosting into my brain. *Little lightning girl. It's what she used to call me, what they called me.*

No. No, it isn't.

Despite the pain, I straighten my spine, standing as tall as I can.

I am not little anymore.

The whispers follow us all the way to the medical station, where a pair of Guardsmen keeps watch at the closed door. They're also watching the ladder, a heavy metal thing reaching up into the ceiling. The only exit and only entrance in this slow bullet of a ship. One of the guards has dark red hair, just like Tristan, though he's nowhere near as tall. The other is built like a boulder, with brown skin, angled eyes, a broad chest, and massive hands better suited to a strongarm. They bow their heads at the sight of me but, to my relief, don't spare me much more than a glance. Instead, they turn their attentions to Kilorn, grinning at him like school friends.

"Back so soon, Warren?" The redhead chuckles, waggling his eyebrows in suggestion. "Lena's gone off her shift."

Lena? Kilorn tenses beneath my arm, but says nothing to betray his discomfort. Instead, he laughs along, grinning. But I know him better than any, enough to see the force behind his smile. To think, he's been spending his time *flirting* while I've been unconscious and Shade lies wounded and bleeding.

"The boy's got enough on his plate without chasing pretty nurses," the boulder says. His deep voice echoes down the passage, probably carrying all the way to Lena's quarters. "Farley's still making rounds, if you're after her," he adds, jabbing a thumb at the door.

"And my brother?" I speak up, disentangling myself from Kilorn's supporting grip. My knees almost buckle, but I stand firm. "Shade Barrow?"

Their smiles fade, stiffening into something more formal. It's almost like being back in the Silver court. The boulder grips the door, spinning the massive wheel lock so he doesn't have to look at me. "He's recovering well, miss, er, my lady."

My stomach drops at the title. I thought I was done with such things.

"Please call me Mare."

"Of course," he replies without any kind of resolve. Though we are both part of the Scarlet Guard, soldiers together in our cause, we are not the same. This man, and many others, will never call me by my given name, no matter how much I want them to.

He swings open the door with a tiny nod, revealing a wide but shallow compartment filled with bunks. Sleeping quarters at one time, but now the stacked beds are full of patients, the single aisle buzzing with men and women in white shifts. Many have clothes spattered with crimson blood, too preoccupied setting a leg or administering medication to notice me limping into their midst.

Kilorn's hand hovers by my waist, ready to catch me should I need him again, but I lean on the bunks instead. If everyone's going to stare at me, I might as well try to walk on my own.

Shade props up against a single thin pillow, supported mostly by the sloping metal wall. He can't possibly be comfortable, but his eyes are closed, and his chest rises and falls in the easy rhythm of sleep. Judging by his leg, suspended from the ceiling of his bunk by a hasty sling, and his bandaged shoulder, he's surely been medicated a few times. The sight of him so broken, even though I thought him dead just yesterday, is shockingly hard to bear.

"We should let him sleep," I murmur to no one in particular, expecting no answer.

"Yes, please do," Shade says without opening his eyes. But his lips quirk into a familiar, mischievous smile. Despite his grim, injured figure, I have to laugh.

The trick is a familiar one. Shade would pretend to sleep through school or our parents' whispered conversations. I have to laugh at the memory, remembering how many little secrets Shade picked up in this particular way. I may have been born a thief, but Shade was born a spy. No wonder he ended up in the Scarlet Guard.

"Eavesdropping on nurses?" My knee cracks as I sit on the side of his bunk, careful not to jostle him. "Have you learned how many bandages they've got squirreled away?"

But instead of laughing at the joke, Shade opens his eyes. He draws Kilorn and me closer with a beckoning hand. "The nurses know more than you think," he says, his gaze flickering toward the far end of the compartment.

I turn to find Farley busying herself over an occupied bunk. The woman in it is out cold, probably drugged, and Farley monitors her pulse closely. In this light, her scar stands out rudely, twisting one side of her mouth into a scowl before cutting down the side of her neck and under her collar. Part of it has split open and was hastily stitched up. Now the only red she wears is the swath of blood across her white nurse's shift and the half-washed stains reaching to her elbows. Another nurse stands at her shoulder, but his shift is clean, and he whispers hurriedly in her ear. She nods occasionally, though her face tightens in anger.

"What have you heard?" Kilorn asks, shifting so that his body blocks Shade entirely. To anyone else, it looks like we're adjusting his bandages.

"We're headed to another base, this time off the coast. Outside Nortan territory."

I strain to remember Julian's old map, but I can't think of much more than the coastline. "An island?"

Shade nods. "Called Tuck. It must not be much, because the Silvers don't even have an outpost there. They've all but forgotten it."

Dread pools in my stomach. The prospect of isolating myself on an island with no means of escape scares me even more than the mersive. "But they know it exists. That's enough."

"Farley seemed confident in the base there."

Kilorn scoffs aloud. "I remember her thinking Naercey was safe too."

"It wasn't her fault we lost Naercey," I say. *It's mine.*

"Maven tricked everyone, Mare," Kilorn replies, nudging my shoulder. "He got past me, you, *and* Farley. We all believed in him."

With his mother to coach him, to read our minds and mold Maven to our hopes, it's no wonder we were all fooled. And now he is king. Now he will fool—and control—our whole world. *What a world that will be, with a monster for its king, and his mother holding his leash.*

But I push through such thoughts. They can wait. "Did Farley say anything else? What about the list? She still has it, doesn't she?"

Shade watches her over my shoulder, careful to keep his voice low. "She does, but she's more concerned with the *others* we're meeting in Tuck, Mom and Dad included." A rush of warmth spreads through me, an invigorating curl of happiness. Shade brightens at the sight of my small but genuine smile, and he takes my hand. "Gisa too, and the lumps we call brothers."

A cord of tension releases in my chest but is soon replaced by another. I tighten my grip on him, one eyebrow raised in question. "*Others?* Who? How can that be?" After the massacre beneath Caesar's Square and the evacuation of Naercey, I didn't think anyone else existed.

But Kilorn and Shade don't share my confusion, electing to exchange furtive glances instead. Yet again, I'm in the dark, and I don't like it one bit. But this time, it's my own brother and best friend keeping secrets, not an evil queen and scheming prince.

Somehow, this hurts more. Scowling, I glare at them both until they realize I'm waiting for answers.

Kilorn grits his teeth and has the good sense to look apologetic. He gestures to Shade. *Passing the blame.* "You know more than I do."

"The Guard likes to play things close to the chest, and rightfully so." Shade adjusts himself, sitting up a little more. He hisses at the motion, clutching at his wounded shoulder, but waves me off before I can help him. "We want to look small, broken, disorganized—"

I can't help but snort, eyeing his bandages. "Well, you're doing a terrific job."

"Don't be cruel, Mare," Shade snaps back, sounding very much like our mother. "I'm trying to tell you that things aren't so bad as they seem. Naercey was not our only stronghold and Farley is not our only leader. In fact, she's not even true Command. She's just a captain. There are others like her—and even more above her."

Judging by the way she orders around her soldiers, I would think Farley was an empress. When I chance another glance at her, she's busy redoing a bandage, all while scolding the nurse who originally set the wound. But my brother's conviction can't be ignored. He knows much more than I do about the Scarlet Guard, and I'm inclined to believe what he says about them is true. There's more to this organization than what I see here. It's encouraging—and frightening.

"The Silvers think they're two steps ahead of us, but they don't even know where we stand," Shade continues, his voice full of fervor. "We seem weak because we want to."

I turn back quickly. "Maven tricked you, trapped you, slaughtered you, and ran you out of your own house. Or are you going to try and tell me that was all part of another plan?"

"Mare—" Kilorn mumbles, putting his shoulder against mine in a display of comfort. But I shove him away. He needs to hear this too.

"I don't care how many secret tunnels and boats and bases you have. You're not going to win against him, not like this." Tears I didn't know I still had sting my eyes, prickling at Maven's memory. It's hard to forget him as he was. *No.* As he pretended to be. The kind, forgotten boy. The shadow of the flame.

"Then what do you suggest, lightning girl?"

Farley's voice shocks through me like my own sparks, setting every nerve on edge. For a brief, blistering second, I stare at my hands knotted in Shade's sheets. *Maybe she'll leave if I don't turn around. Maybe she'll let me be.*

Don't be such a fool, Mare Barrow.

"Fight fire with fire," I tell her as I stand. Her height used to intimidate me. Now glaring up at her feels natural and familiar.

"Is that some kind of Silver joke?" she sneers, crossing her arms.

"Do I look like I'm joking?"

She doesn't reply, and that's answer enough. In her silence, I realize the rest of the compartment has gone quiet. Even the injured stifle their pain to watch the lightning girl challenge their captain.

"You thrive on looking weak and striking hard, yes? Well, they do everything they can to look strong, to seem invincible. But in the arena, I proved they are not." *Again, stronger, so everyone can hear you.* I call on the firm voice Lady Blonos brought to life in me. "They are *not* invincible."

Farley isn't stupid and finds it easy to follow my train of thought. "You're stronger than they are," she says, matter-of-fact. Her eyes stray to Shade, lying tense in his bunk. "And you're not the only one who is."

I nod sharply, pleased that she already knows what I want. "Hundreds of names, hundreds of Reds with abilities. Stronger, faster, better than they are, with blood as Red as the dawn." My breath catches, as if it knows it stands on the edge of the future. "Maven will try to kill them, but if we get to them first, they could be—"

"The greatest army this world has ever seen." Farley's eyes glass at the thought. "An army of newbloods."

When she smiles, her scar strains against its stitches, threatening to split open again. Her grin widens. She doesn't mind the pain.

But I certainly do. I suppose I always will.

FOUR

Farley's not as tall as Kilorn, but her steps are faster, more deliberate, and harder to keep up with. I do my best, almost jogging to match her pace through the mersive corridor. Like before, the Guardsmen jump out of our way, but now they salute her as we pass, clasping hands to their chest or fingers to their brow. I must say Farley cuts an impressive figure, wearing her scars and wounds like jewels. She doesn't seem to mind the blood on her shift, absently wiping her hands against it. Some of it belongs to Shade. She dug the bullet out of his shoulder without blinking.

"We didn't lock him up, if that's what you think," she says lightly, as if talk of imprisoning Cal is casual gossip.

I'm not stupid enough to rise to that bait, not now. She's feeling me out, testing my reaction, my *allegiance*. But I'm no longer the girl who begged for her help. I'm not so easily read anymore. I've lived on a razor wire, balancing lie after lie, hiding myself. It's nothing to do the same now and bury my thoughts deep down.

So I laugh instead, pasting on the smile I perfected in Elara's court.

"I can tell. Nothing's been melted," I reply, gesturing to the metal walls.

I read her as she tries to read me. She masks her expression well, but surprise still flickers in her eyes. Surprise and *curiosity*.

I haven't forgotten the way she treated Cal on the train—with shackles, armed guards, and disdain. And he took it like a kicked dog. After his brother's betrayal and his father's murder, he had no fight inside him. I didn't blame him. But Farley doesn't know his heart—or his strength—like I do. She doesn't know how dangerous he really is. *Or how dangerous I am, for that matter.* Even now, despite my many injuries, I feel power deep inside, calling out to the electricity pulsing through the mersive. I could control it if I wanted. I could shut this whole thing down. I could drown us all. The lethal idea makes me blush, embarrassed by such thoughts. But they are a comfort all the same. I'm the greatest weapon of all on a ship full of warriors, and they don't seem to know it.

We seem weak because we want to. Shade was talking about the Guard when he said that, explaining their motives. Now I wonder if he wasn't also trying to convey a message. Like words hidden in a letter long ago.

Cal's bunk room is at the far end of the mersive, tucked away from the bustle of the rest of the vessel. His door is nearly hidden behind a twist of pipes and empty crates stamped with *Archeon, Haven, Corvium, Harbor Bay, Delphie,* and even *Belleum* from Piedmont to the south. What the crates once held, I can't say, but the names of the Silver cities send a twinge down my spine. *Stolen.* Farley notices me staring at the crates but doesn't bother to explain. Despite our shaky agreement over what she calls "newbloods," I still haven't entered her inner circle of secrets. I suppose Cal has something to do with that.

Whatever powers the ship, a massive generator by the feel of it, rumbles beneath my feet, vibrating into my bones. I wrinkle my nose in distaste. Farley might not have locked Cal up, but she's certainly not being kind either. Between the noise and the shaking sensation, I wonder if Cal was able to sleep at all.

"I suppose this is the only place you could put him?" I ask, glaring at the cramped corner.

She shrugs, banging a hand on his door. "The prince hasn't complained."

We don't wait long, though I'd very much like the time to collect myself. Instead, the wheel lock spins in seconds, clanking round at great speed. The iron hinges grate, screaming, and Cal pulls open the door.

I'm not surprised to see him standing tall, ignoring his own aches. After a lifetime preparing to be a warrior, he's used to cuts and bruises. But the scars within are something he doesn't know how to hide. He avoids my gaze, focusing on Farley, who doesn't notice or doesn't care about the prince with a shattered heart. Suddenly my wounds seem a bit easier to bear.

"Captain Farley," he says, as if she's disturbed him at dinnertime. He uses annoyance to mask his pain.

Farley won't stand for it and tosses her short hair with a sniff. She even reaches to close the door. "Oh, did you not want a visitor? How rude of me."

I'm quietly glad I didn't let Kilorn tag along. He'd be even worse to Cal, having hated him since they first met back in the Stilts.

"Farley," I tell her through gritted teeth. My hand stops the door short. To my delight—and distaste—she flinches away from my touch. She flushes horribly, embarrassed with herself and her fear. Despite her tough exterior, she's just like her soldiers. Afraid of the lightning girl. "I think we're fine from here."

Something twitches in her face, a twinge of irritation as much with herself as with me. But she nods, grateful to be out of my presence. With one last daggered glance at Cal, she turns and disappears back down the corridor. Her barked orders echo for a moment, indecipherable but strong.

Cal and I stare after her, then at the walls, then at the floor, then at our feet, afraid to look at each other. Afraid to remember the last few days. The last time we watched each other across a doorway, dancing lessons and a stolen kiss followed. That might as well be another life. *Because it was. He danced with Mareena, the lost princess, and Mareena is dead.*

But her memories remain. When I walk past, my shoulder brushing one firm arm, I remember the feel and smell and taste of him. Heat and wood smoke and sunrise, but no longer. Cal smells like blood, his skin is ice, and I tell myself I don't want to taste him ever again.

"They've been treating you well?" I speak first, reaching for an easy topic. One glance around his small yet clean compartment is answer enough, but I might as well fill the silence.

"Yes," he says, still hovering by the open door. Debating whether to shut it.

My eyes land on a panel in the wall, pried back to reveal a tangle of wires and switches beneath. I can't help but smile softly. Cal's been tinkering.

"You think that's smart? One wrong wire . . ."

That draws a weak but still comforting smile from him. "I've been fooling with circuitry for half my life. Don't worry, I know what I'm doing."

Both of us ignore the double meaning, letting it slide past.

He finally decides to shut the door, though he leaves it unlocked. One hand rests on the metal wall, fingers splayed, looking for something to hold on to. The flame-maker bracelet still winks on his wrist, bright silver against dull, hard gray. He notes my gaze and pulls down one stained sleeve; I guess no one thought to give him a change of clothes.

"As long as I stay out of sight, I don't think anyone will bother with me," he says, and goes back to fiddling with the open panel. "It's kind of nice." But the joke is hollow.

"I'll make sure it stays that way. If that's what you want," I add quickly. In truth, I have no idea what Cal wants now. *Beyond vengeance. The one thing we still have in common.*

He quirks an eyebrow at me, almost amused. "Oh, is the lightning girl in charge now?" He doesn't give me a chance to respond to the jibe, closing the distance between us in a single long step. "I get the feeling you're just as cornered as me." His eyes narrow. "Only you don't seem to know it."

I flush, feeling angry—and embarrassed. "Cornered? I'm not the one hiding in a closet."

"No, you're too busy being put on parade." He leans forward, and the familiar heat between us returns. *"Again."*

Part of me wants to slap him. "My brother would *never*—"

"I thought my brother would *never*, and look where that got us!" he thunders, throwing his arms wide. The tips of his fingers touch either wall, scraping up against the prison he's found himself in. *The prison I put him in.* And he's caged me in with him, whether he knows it or not.

Blazing heat flares from his body, and I have to step back a little. He doesn't miss the action and deflates, letting his eyes and arms drop. "Sorry," he bites out, brushing a lock of black hair off his forehead.

"Never apologize to me. I don't deserve it."

He glances at me sidelong, his eyes dark and wide, but he doesn't argue.

Heaving a breath, I lean back against the far wall. The space between us gapes like open jaws. "What do you know about a place called Tuck?"

Grateful for the change in conversation, he pulls himself together, retreating into a prince's persona. Even without a crown, he seems regal, with perfect posture and his hands folded behind his back. "Tuck?" he repeats, thinking hard. A crease forms between his thick, dark brows. The longer it takes him to speak, the better I feel. If he doesn't know about the island, then few else will. "Is that where we're going?"

"It is." *I think.* A cold thought ripples through me, remembering Julian's lessons hard learned in the court and the arena. *Anyone can betray anyone.* "According to Shade."

Cal lets my uncertainty hang in the air, kind enough not to prod at it. "I think it's an island," he finally says. "One of several off the coast. It's not Nortan territory. Nothing to warrant a settlement or base, not even for defense. It's just open ocean out there."

A bit of the weight on my shoulders lifts. We'll be safe for now. "Good, good."

"Your brother, he's like you." It's not a question. "Different."

"He is." What else is there to say?

"And he's all right? I remember he was injured."

Even without an army, Cal is still a general, caring for the soldiers and the wounded. "He's fine, thank you. Took a few bullets for me, but he's recovering well."

At the mention of bullets, Cal's eyes flicker over me, finally allowing himself to look at me fully. He lingers on my scraped face and the dried blood around my ears. "And you?"

"I've had worse."

"Yes, we have."

We lapse into silence, not daring to speak further. But we still continue to stare at each other. Suddenly his presence is difficult to stand. And yet I don't want to go.

The mersive has other ideas.

Beneath my feet, the generator shudders, its pounding pulse changing rhythm. "We're almost there," I mutter, sensing electricity flow or ebb to different parts of the craft.

Cal doesn't feel it yet, unable to, but he doesn't question my instincts. He knows my abilities firsthand, better than anyone on the ship. Better than my own family. For now, at least. Mom, Dad, Gisa, the boys, they're waiting for me on the island. I'll see them soon. They're here. They're *safe*.

But how long I'll be with them, I don't know. I won't be able to stay on the island, not if I want to do something for the newbloods. I'll have to go back to Norta, use whatever and whoever Farley can give me, to try and find them. It already seems impossible. I don't even want to think about it. And yet my mind buzzes, trying to form a plan.

An alarm sounds overhead, synchronizing with a yellow light that starts to flash over Cal's door. "Amazing," I hear him mutter, distracted for a moment by the great machine all around us. I don't doubt he wanted to explore, but there's no room for the inquisitive prince here. The boy who buried himself in manuals and built cycles from scratch has no place in this world. *I killed him, just as I killed Mareena.*

Despite Cal's mechanically inclined mind and my own electrical sense, we have no idea what comes next. When the mersive angles, nosing up out of the depths of the ocean, the whole room tips. The surprise of it knocks us both off our feet. We collide with the wall and each other. Our wounds bang together, drawing pained hisses from us both.

The feel of him hurts more than anything else, a deep stab of memory, and I scramble away quickly.

Wincing, I rub one of my many bruises. "Where's Sara Skonos when you need her," I grumble, wishing for the skin healer who could mend us both. She could chase away the aches with a single touch, returning us both to fighting form.

More pain crosses Cal's face, but not from his injuries. *Well done, Mare. Wonderful job, bringing up the woman who knew his mother was murdered by the queen. The woman no one believed.* "Sorry, I didn't mean—"

He waves me off and finds his feet, one arm pressed against the wall for balance. "It's fine. She's—" The words are thick, stilted. "I chose not to listen to her. I didn't *want* to listen. That was my fault."

I met Sara Skonos only once, when Evangeline almost exposed me to our entire training session. Julian summoned her—Julian, who *loved* her—and watched as she mended my bloody face and bruised back. Her eyes were sad, her cheeks hollow, her tongue missing entirely. Taken for words spoken against the queen, for a truth no one believed. *Elara killed Cal's mother, Coriane the Singer Queen. Julian's own sister, Sara's best friend. And no one seemed to mind. It was so much easier to look away.*

Maven was there too, hating Sara with every breath. I know now that was a crack in his shield, revealing who he truly was beneath practiced words and gentle smiles. Like Cal, I didn't see what was right in front of me.

Like Julian, she is probably dead already.

Suddenly the metal walls and the noise and the popping of my ears are too much.

"I need to get off this thing."

Despite the strange angle of the room and the persistent ringing in my head, my feet know what to do. They have not forgotten the mud of the Stilts, the nights spent in alleys, or the obstacle courses of Training. I wrench the door open, gasping for breath like a girl drowned. But the stale, filtered air of the mersive offers me no respite. I need the smell of trees, water, spring rains, even summer heat or winter snow. *Something* to remind me of the world beyond this suffocating tin can.

Cal gives me a head start before following, his footsteps heavy and slow behind me. He's not trying to catch up, but give me space. If only Kilorn could do the same.

He approaches from farther down the corridor, using handholds and wheel locks to ease himself down the angled craft. His smile fades at the sight of Cal, replaced not by a scowl but by cold indifference. I suppose he thinks ignoring the prince will anger him more than outright hostility. Or perhaps Kilorn doesn't want to test a human flamethrower in such close quarters.

"We're surfacing," he says, reaching my side.

I tighten my grip on a nearby grate, using it to steady myself. "You don't say?"

Kilorn grins, leaning against the wall in front of me. He plants his feet on either side of mine, a challenge if there ever was one. I feel Cal's heat behind me, but the prince seems to be taking the indifferent path as well, and says nothing.

I won't be a piece in whatever game they're playing. I've done that enough for a lifetime. "How's what's-her-name? Lena?"

The name hits Kilorn like a slap. His grin slackens, one side of his mouth drooping. "She's fine, I guess."

"That's good, Kilorn." I give him a friendly, if condescending, pat on the shoulder. The deflection works perfectly. "We should be making friends."

The mersive levels out beneath us, but no one stumbles. Not even

Cal, who has nowhere near my balance or Kilorn's sea legs, hard earned on a fishing boat. He's taut as a wire, waiting for me to take the lead. It should make me laugh, the thought of a prince deferring to me, but I'm too cold and worn to do much of anything but carry on.

So I do. Down the corridor, with Cal and Kilorn in tow, to the throng of Guardsmen waiting by the ladder that brought us down here in the first place. The wounded go first, tied onto makeshift stretchers and hoisted up into the open night. Farley supervises, her shift even bloodier than before. She makes for a grim sight, tightening bandages, with a syringe between her teeth. A few of the worse off get shots as they pass, medication to help with the pain of being moved up the narrow tube. Shade is the last of the injured, leaning heavily on the two Guardsmen who teased Kilorn about the nurse. I would push through to him, but the crowd is too tight, and I don't want any more attention today. Still too weak to teleport, he has to fumble on one leg and blushes furiously when Farley straps him onto a stretcher. I can't hear what she says to him, but it calms him somewhat. He even waves off her syringe, instead gritting his teeth against the jarring pain of being hoisted up the ladder. Once Shade is safely carried up, the process goes much faster. One after the other, Guardsmen follow one another up the ladder, slowly clearing the corridor. Many of them are nurses, men and women marked by white shifts with varying degrees of bloodstains.

I don't waste time waving others ahead, faking politeness like a lady should. We're all going to the same place. So when the crowd clears a little, the ladder opening to me, I hurry forward. Cal follows, and his presence combined with mine parts the Guardsmen like a knife. They step back quickly, some even stumbling, to give us our space. Only Farley stands firm, one hand around the ladder. To my surprise, she offers Cal and me a nod. *Both* of us.

That should've been my first warning.

The steps on the ladder burn in my muscles, still strained from Naercey, the arena, and my capture. I can hear a strange howling up above, but it doesn't deter me in the slightest. I need to get out of the mersive, as fast as possible.

My last glimpse of the mersive, looking back over my shoulder, is strange, angling over Farley and into the medical station. There are wounded still in there, motionless beneath their blankets. *No, not wounded,* I realize as I pull myself up. *Dead.*

Higher up the ladder, the wind sounds, and a bit of water drips down. Nothing to bother with, I assume, until I reach the top and the open circle of darkness. A storm howls so strongly that the rain pelts sideways, missing most of the tube and ladder. It stings against my scraped face, drenching me in seconds. *Autumn storms.* Though I cannot recall a storm so brutal as this. It blows through me, filling my mouth with rain and biting, salty spray. Luckily, the mersive is tightly anchored to a dock I can barely see, and it holds firm against the roiling gray waves below.

"This way!" a familiar voice yells in my ear, guiding me off the ladder and onto the mersive hull slick with rain and seawater. Through the darkness, I can barely see the soldier leading me, but his massive bulk and his voice are easy to place.

"Bree!" I close my hand on his, feeling the calluses of my oldest brother's grip. He walks like an anchor, heavy and slow, helping me off the mersive and onto the dock. It's not much better, metal eaten with rust, but it leads to land and that's all I care about. Land and *warmth,* a welcome respite after the cold depths of the ocean and my memories.

No one helps Cal down from the mersive, but he does fine on his own. Again, he's careful to keep some distance, walking a few respectable paces behind us. I'm sure he hasn't forgotten his first meeting with

Bree back in the Stilts, when my brother was anything but polite. In truth, none of the Barrows cared for Cal, except Mom and maybe Gisa. But they didn't know who he was then. Should be an interesting reunion.

The storm makes Tuck difficult to see, but I can tell the island is small, covered in dunes and tall grass as tumultuous as the waves. A crack of lightning out on the water illuminates the night for a moment, showing the path in front of us. Now out in the open, without the cramped walls of the mersive or the Undertrain, I can see we number less than thirty, including the wounded. They head for two flat, concrete buildings where the dock meets land. A few structures stand out on the gentle hill above us, looking like bunkers or barracks. But what lies beyond them, I can't say. The next bolt of lightning, closer this time, shivers delightfully in my nerves. Bree mistakes it for cold, and draws me closer, draping one heavy arm across my shoulders. His weight makes it hard to walk, but I endure.

The end of the dock cannot come fast enough. Soon I'll be inside, dry, on solid ground, and reunited with the Barrows after far too long. The prospect is enough to get me through the bustle of wet activity. Nurses load the wounded onto an old transport, its storage bed covered in waterproof canvas. It was certainly stolen, as was everything else. The two buildings on land are hangars, their doors ajar enough to reveal more transports waiting inside. There's even a few boats anchored to the dock, bobbing in the gray waves as they ride out the storm. Everything is mismatched—outdated transports in varying sizes, sleek new boats, some painted silver, black, one green. Stolen or hijacked or both. I even recognize the clouded gray and blue, the Nortan navy colors, on one boat. Tuck is like a much larger version of Will Whistle's old wagon, packed with bits and pieces of trade and thievery.

The medical transport putters off before we reach it, fighting through the rain and up the sandy road. Only Bree's nonchalance keeps me from quickening my pace. He isn't worried about Shade, or what lies at the top of the hill, so I try not to be too.

Cal doesn't share my sentiment and finally speeds up so he can walk next to me. It's the storm or the darkness, or maybe simply his silver blood making him look so pale and afraid. "This can't last," he mutters, low enough so only I can hear.

"What's that, Prince?" Bree says, his voice a dull roar. I nudge him in the ribs, but it doesn't do much more than bruise my elbow. "No matter, we'll know soon enough."

His tone is worse than his words. Cold, brutal, so unlike the laughing brother I used to know. The Guard has changed him too. "Bree, what are you talking about?"

Cal already knows and stops in his tracks, his eyes on me. The wind musses his hair, pasting it to his forehead. His bronze eyes darken with fear, and my stomach churns at the sight. *Not again,* I plead. *Tell me I haven't walked into another trap.*

One of the hangars looms behind him, its doors opening wide on strangely quiet hinges. Too many soldiers to count step forward in unison, as regimented as any legion, their guns ready and eyes bright in the rain. Their leader might as well be a shiver, with almost white-blond hair and an icy disposition. But he's red-blooded as I am—one of his eyes is clouded crimson, bleeding beneath the lens.

"Bree, what is this?!" I yell, rounding on my brother with a visceral snarl. Instead, he takes my hands in his, and not gently. He holds me firm, using his superior strength to keep me from pulling away. If he were anyone else, I would shock him good. But this is my brother. I can't do that to him, I *won't.*

"Bree, *let me go!*"

"We won't hurt him," he says, repeating it over and over. "We're not going to hurt him, I promise you."

So this isn't my cage. But that doesn't calm me at all. If anything, it makes me more angry and desperate.

When I look back, Cal's fists are aflame, his arms stretched wide to face the blood-eyed man. "Well?" he growls in challenge, sounding more like an animal than a man. *A cornered animal.*

Too many guns, even for Cal. They'll shoot him if they must. It might even be what they want. An excuse to kill the fallen prince. Part of me, most of me, knows they would be justified in this. Cal was a hunter of the Scarlet Guard, essentially guaranteeing Tristan's death, Walsh's suicide, and Farley's torture. Soldiers killed at his orders, wiping out most of Farley's rebel force. And who knows how many he's sent to die on the war front, trading Red soldiers for a few measly miles of the Lakelands. He owes no allegiance to the cause. He is a danger to the Scarlet Guard.

But he is a weapon as well as I am, one we can use in the days to come. For the newbloods, against Maven, a torch to help lift the darkness.

"He can't fight out of this, Mare." That's Kilorn, choosing the worst of moments to sidle back. He whispers in my ear, acting like his closeness can influence me. "He'll die if he tries."

His logic is hard to ignore.

"On your knees, Tiberias," the blood-eyed man says, taking bold steps toward the flaming prince. Steam rises from his fire, as if the storm is trying to stamp him out. "Hands behind your head."

Cal does neither, and he flinches at the mention of his birth name. He stands firm, strong, proud, though he knows the battle is lost.

Once he might have surrendered, trying to save his own skin. Now he believes that skin worthless. Only I seem to think otherwise.

"Cal, do as he says."

The wind carries my voice so that the whole hangar hears. I'm afraid they can hear my heart too, hammering like a drum in my chest.

"*Cal*."

Slowly, reluctantly, a statue crumbling to dust, Cal sinks to his knees and his fire sputters out. He did the same thing yesterday, kneeling next to his father's decapitated corpse.

The blood-eyed man grins, his teeth gleaming and straight. He stands over Cal with relish, enjoying the sight of a prince at his feet. Enjoying the *power* it gives him.

But I am the lightning girl, and he knows nothing of true power.

ACKNOWLEDGMENTS

My deepest thanks to the tireless team who keeps the Red Queen machine moving forward. The New Leaf squad, especially Suzie Townsend, Pouya Shahbazian, Danielle Barthel, Jackie Lindert, Kathleen Ortiz, and Jess Dallow, who keep me sane, organized, and are integral in every aspect of my publishing career. Everyone at Harper-Teen, from editor Kristen "Kneel or Bleed" Pettit to the epic Margot Wood to Elizabeth Lynch, who keeps us all working. The film team at Benderspink, Daniel, JC, the Jakes. My family and friends, who tolerate me through the hardest parts of writing. And, of course, every single teacher, librarian, bookseller, fellow author, blogger, journalist, and reader who put *Red Queen* on a shelf or in the hand of someone else. Everything counts, everything helps, and I'm so eternally grateful to all of you!

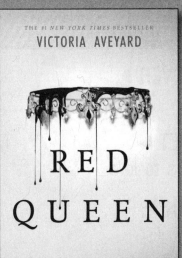

RED QUEEN
FAN ART

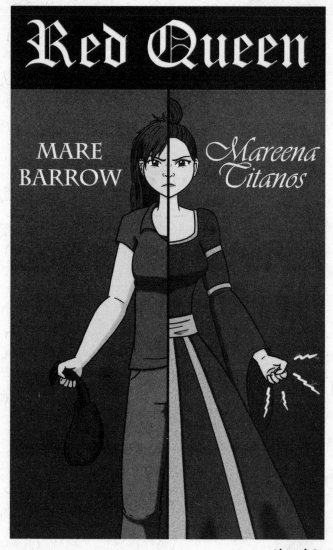

Red Queen

MARE BARROW · *Mareena Titanos*

Abigail Casey
18 • Ohio, USA

Caterina Caccavale
21 • Nola, Italy

Allarica
22 • Manila, Philippines

Echo Rose
15 • Born and raised in Chengdu, China;
currently living in Quebec, Canada

Marga H. Garcia
24 • Born and raised in Valladolid, Spain;
currently living in Paris, France

Grace Fong

26 • California, USA

Miyako Molinelli

20 • Vermont, USA

THE KINGDOM OF NORTA
& THE SURROUNDING LANDS

Q&A WITH
VICTORIA AVEYARD

1. Would anyone in your life recognize themselves in one of the characters in the Red Queen world? If so, how would they feel about that?

   The character of Farley was definitely based on a friend of mine, and she knows it! Same personality, same appearance. But in real life, she has fairy-princess hair that I'm always jealous of, so I had Farley cut off all her hair in the book. A bit of vengeance on my part.

2. Mare is obviously a beloved, strong female protagonist. Why do you feel it's important to represent these kinds of characters in YA fiction? Do you see yourself in Mare?

   I think we emulate what we see in our stories, but at the same time, our stories are a direct mirror of the time they're made in, and what that time values or needs. Not only do readers today want to see these characters in their fiction, they need to. And while strong female characters have been around for centuries, millennia even, only now are they considered viable and popular on a grand scale. I'm so pleased that teenagers now have a slew of heroines to gorge themselves on, particularly when I remember myself as a kid, latching on to Princess Leia, Hermione Granger, and Arwen, looking for strong females and not finding many. And, of course, I put some of myself in Mare (mostly the bad bits), but also made much of her what I want to be.

3. If you could drop a character from any other fantasy world into Mare's world, who would you pick?

Oh, good question. I guess I'd love for Professor X to come to town and teach the Silvers a lesson about equality and tolerance. Plus, he'd kick Elara's ass in a great mind-control battle.

4. How did you learn about some of the more technical elements in the Red Queen series, like weaponry and military strategy? Do you do a lot of research before you start writing?

Not consciously, but I'm a big fan of action movies, history, and adventure books, so I guess it was kind of absorbed over the course of a life spent watching Independence Day *and* Saving Private Ryan. *I'm a big fan of medieval warfare, but I actually had to steer away from a lot of my medieval military knowledge because it simply didn't fit the world and wars of* Red Queen. *Traditional pitched battle would not fit, so I erred on the side of trench warfare. The major bit of military research I remember doing was for book 2, and that was just looking at submarine schematics so I knew what to picture while writing several scenes. I think the most hard research I did was into superhuman abilities, trying to find ones that were unique, and figuring out ways to twist familiar ones into something different.*

5. If Mare, Cal, Maven, Kilorn, and Evangeline were characters in a YA book set in a modern-day high school, what would they be like? Would there be a love triangle?

I love this question. Never had it before, and it's a kick to think about. Mare would probably cut class a lot, but do well in the few classes she liked and probably find her way onto the debate team. Also track and cross-country. Cal would be so basic, a total good boy balancing football, dance team, a 4.0, and probably applying to West Point to get away from his wacko stepmom. Maven is a bit tricky. I think he'd be a floater, with friends in lots of social groups, totally under the radar in his brother's shadow, waiting for the second Cal graduates and leaves. I can see him being really quiet, playing soccer, and writing anonymous Gossip Girl-esque articles in the school newspaper. Kilorn would live in shop and cooking class, terrible at academics but would try his best to keep up his GPA so he could stay on the track team with Mare. And Evangeline would be straight-up wonder girl. Captain of three sports (soccer, volleyball, lacrosse), all AP classes, laser focused on getting into an Ivy League school to study political science. On track to run for office by 30.

6. What are your writing-space essentials when you sit down to write a new book?

Desk. Coffee. Music. Time. The last two are my biggest needs. I'm very precious and silly about needing lots of time when I write. If I know I have to be somewhere in two hours, it's very difficult for me to buckle down and get any creative work done. And I love to make playlists for different projects.

7. Do you have a quote or a mantra that helps you through your writing process?

Several, all learned from my college professors when I was studying screen-writing at the University of Southern California. First, finish. Get to the end. Don't get tripped up editing prematurely, or you'll never finish what you're working on. Power through, even if this scene is bad and that scene needs to be reworked. Second, the audience can believe one unbelievable thing. Build everything else off that.

8. In addition to being a bestselling author, you're also a screenwriter. What kinds of movies inspire you?

I'm such a film dork. A good movie has me leaving the theater with stars in my eyes and my heart bursting with excitement for what could be. I'm a child of Spielberg and Lucas, first and foremost. Star Wars, Jurassic Park, ET, Raiders, *etc., are what I grew up with, and what I constantly aspire to. And* The Lord of the Rings *(both Jackson and Tolkien) made me realize that stories were what I had to do with my life. I'm big into the summer-movie scene. Blockbusters are my hands-down favorite, followed by historical epics. I love movies like* Pirates of the Caribbean, Independence Day, Armageddon, *the Marvel and DC movies,* Gladiator, Pacific Rim, Mad Max: Fury Road— *larger-than-life movies that are a roller coaster from start to finish, usually with big sci-fi or fantasy worlds behind them. I'm also a sucker for crime movies—*Goodfellas, The Godfather, The Departed. *Oh, and Disney movies. I could go on forever about the movies I love. Television too. Oh, man.*

9. What do you look for in a YA book, fantasy or otherwise? What genres and topics pull you in?

Big worlds. I want maps, family trees, a place and time I can drown in. I'm all about genre-at-large (fantasy, sci-fi, paranormal, etc.) and the higher the stakes, the better. I want the world at stake. But at the same time, I'm a sucker for high school romance, so long as it feels like this small town exists. Basically, keep me entertained, keep me hooked. I'm pretty shallow in my tastes. I need two of the following: explosions, dragons, hot guys, badass women.

10. What has surprised you the most about the experience of becoming a published (bestselling!) author?

Basically every facet of my current reality is surprising. I was surprised when I finished the first draft of Red Queen, *when an agent signed me, when a publishing company bought it, and when it subsequently debuted at #1 on the* New York Times *bestseller list. I'm surprised I get to wake up in the morning, do what I love, and get paid for it. Honestly, it's all a bit of a dream.*

11. Did you love to read when you were a kid? What's one book you wish you could go back and give to your younger self?

My not-so-secret shame: I didn't read The Lord of the Rings *until I saw the first movie in 2001. Yeah, I was only eleven, but the way that book captured my heart and soul was nothing short of magic, and I wish I'd gotten my hands on it sooner. I also didn't read* A Game of Thrones *until a few months before the show started and, again, wish I had read it sooner. Actually, not really. Then I would've had to wait even longer between books.*

12. Describe the Red Queen fandom in three words.

Lovely, creative, suspicious (AS THEY SHOULD BE. ANYONE CAN BETRAY ANYONE.).

13. What can you tell us about what's to come for Mare?

Her road gets rockier, her world darker. She's been through so much, and it's going to show. And there are some things a person can't forget and can't recover from. Like the fandom, she's going to have a very difficult time trusting anyone ever again.